Yours, Constance

EMILY HAYSE

To anyone who has walked the long road of grief

and

*to the Unshakable Hayse Kids and our fifth wheel.
Just look at us all now.*

Contents

Prologue

"LADIES AND GENTLEMEN, I have a special surprise for you." The stage magician's voice shot through the empty room as a lone spotlight snapped on, as sharp and sudden as his voice.

A small golden box sat alone in the middle of a table. Beneath it, a black cloth covered the table to the floorboards of the stage.

The magician strode into the light, gesturing to the box with a gloved hand.

You could have heard a pin drop in that theater, and I mean that. Everyone hung on his words as if he'd cast a real spell over us.

Sydney Whittington was all the rage: tall, muscular, mysterious. Outspoken in politics, a master on the stage.

No one knew what he was doing or thinking at any given time.

And this—all his acts were spoken of widely, but this was one I did not recognize.

"I would like a volunteer from the audience. Not a plant." His green eyes flicked sternly over the audience, over the box seats above him.

His gloved hand pointed out an older gentleman, Warner Beckham, who'd made his fortune in banking, and beckoned him on stage. A gasp broke out through the audience.

It is the easiest thing to plant someone. A plant could be anyone, really. But Mr. Beckham? That would be calling into question his way of life and profession for the last fifty years. It couldn't be.

"Inspect this box," commanded Sydney. "Look it over carefully. Is it corporeal? Do you see any marks or hooks on it that may give you cause to believe it part of an illusion?"

The old man took his time. It was solid in his hands. From my seat close by the stage I could hear the sound of tempered metal against his fingertips.

"It is a gold box, nothing more," announced Beckham. "Smooth, and pure gold if I am not mistaken."

"Thank you." Sydney gestured to release him and

waited, patient and still as a statue, until Mr. Beckham had left.

"I am about to do something that has never been seen in this hall or any like it," he declared, pulling off one glove, holding his bare hand over the box.

One pass, two passes, and the box began to glow. Not like a lantern, with a single, steady light, but as if the gold itself were turning to millions of tiny burning stars.

He hadn't touched the box. No one had. And there had been nothing to divert the attention.

It had the look and smell of faerie magic, the sort of thing that was whispered about but not really believed in my circles.

That was the frightening thing about Sydney Whittington. A charlatan might tout the supposed use of faerie magic from the beginning. A thing like that you'd use to your advantage, especially with rumors that blood of the Old Folk ran in your family.

But he had never mentioned it once.

The glowing lights reflected off his face, off his glinting green eyes, against his dark, slick hair that caught the spotlight and threw it back up defiantly.

Small wonder half the girls—and women, too—in my circles found him incomparably handsome.

His hand was held over the box, now with straining effort, as if he were trying to hold the lights back.

We held our breath.

With his fingers still hovering, he pulled the gold upwards, stealing it from the box, and suddenly a flash of light overpowered the stage.

The audience gasped aloud, an involuntary reaction.

The gold was free, in tiny motes of gold dust, the smoke trickling across the stage and wafting upwards.

The box was nowhere to be seen.

But the act was not over. Sydney was reaching for the dust, his arms outstretched.

And that's when heavy-booted footsteps broke the spell.

"Sydney Whittington, you are under arrest." Five men strode out onto the stage, through the crawling smoke.

At first, I thought it was part of the act. Until one of them struck him in the face and a second seized his shoulder and shoved him to the stage boards.

The crowd erupted. Women screamed, men shouted, and there was a rush of bodies towards the stage, like a sea swell.

Two policemen stepped forward with their guns;

objects were being thrown, people were fleeing the theater.

They were handcuffing Sydney tightly, checking his pockets as he lay face-down on the floor.

The smoke crawled over them all, turning the entire spectacle into something out of a distant nightmare.

I don't remember getting to my feet, but I was standing. Opera glasses in my numb fingers, watching it all madly, glitteringly, unfold.

I was neither afraid nor morbidly curious. I was strangely outside of it all, yet wrapped in it too.

The smoke drifting through the air reached me, touched my fingertips with a damp chill.

It wasn't smoke at all. It was mist.

One

The inhabitants of Faerie are impossible to spot in the world of man—and there are many doorways to and from, many of them bright and wonderful.

—A History of Faerie and the Folk

I USED TO HATE SNOW. I used to dread its arrival, the small, gentle flakes falling like quiet threats, promising the coming of tearing, howling winds that would soon drive it against the windows, choke the roads, turn the days dull and short.

I hated it more after it took my sister.

We weren't close, my sister and I. She and I were

wild and free in our own ways, I with my parties and gowns, and she with her friends and their frequent outings to town, sometimes staying out so late that the edges of dawn beat her home.

So on that early spring day, when she didn't come home and a policeman with a grim, white face came instead, I didn't know what to feel.

Mother always said her reckless living—reckless driving, in this case—would get her killed, but when you are young, you somehow think it will not happen to you.

I am sure Marge felt that way.

I didn't cry. Not at the news, not at the funeral, though her friends did—copiously. I couldn't. The tears weren't there and neither were my feelings.

After the funeral, I resolved to go to every party I could find.

It was summer then, when everything started: that beautiful, fateful, golden season. And none of it would have happened if it weren't for the two scandals, one right on top of the other.

The first one happened at the Archon theater, on June the thirteenth, when at a special exhibition, the renowned stage magician Sydney Whittington was violently arrested in the middle of his final act.

His father, with whom he'd just had a terrible fight, had died under suspicious circumstances that night, and all fingers had pointed at him.

The second scandal was that the police force lost him on the way to the station. He'd vanished, as it were, into thin air.

However, those things together lit a single spark, ready to fall on the dry tinder of society.

Sixteen-year-old Ella Whittington, Sydney's only sibling, pure and untouched by the cold, cruel world, became the wealthiest heiress in the whole country overnight.

And when society finds a new darling, the parties go mad.

That was the world I stepped into—perfectly timed, I'd thought—when I resolved to drown my hollowness in bright lights, loud music, and lurid gossip.

I wasn't fooling myself, really. I was bored. Horribly, intolerably bored. Bored of parties, of rich food and expensive drink, and each estate, each host trying to outdo the last in lavish, wasteful opulence.

I was bored of it all.

Yet I went, secretly hating the to-do as I did. I think I hoped that somehow the wild extravagance would stir me up, make me feel at least a little more life than I felt. Which, really, was none at all.

I remember the moment that first invitation came. I nearly threw it out. I had been lounging on the sofa in the sunroom, a book hanging from my indifferent fingers, inches from crashing to the cool marble floor.

I wished I could be on the floor. At least I would have been less hot.

A knock came at the door, echoing across the marble.

"Come in."

A servant came in, carrying a letter tray.

"This just arrived, miss. You said you wanted to see any mail as soon as it came."

I sat up, tossing the volume to the foot of the sofa. "Let me see it." I reached into the small tray and pulled out a neat invitation, ripping it open.

"You're reading *A History of Faerie and the Folk*, miss?" Her voice was suddenly keen, alive.

"Don't get excited. I don't believe it," I retorted quickly. "It's sentimentalist tosh. I am bored, that is all."

The invitation was from the Trentons at Featherton

Square, an ostentatious waste of new money on the heights above the city.

That meant the party would be expensive without the snobbery of old money. And that sort of party was the easiest place to have a good time.

"Regina," I said slowly, fingering the edge of the invitation, toying with the idea of tearing it, just because I could. "Any word from the store downtown?"

"The dress arrived moments ago. I was going to mention it before I left."

"Hm. Have it sent up to my room straight away."

"Yes, miss." She nodded respectfully and turned to leave.

"And Regina?"

"Miss?"

"You can believe in the faerie world if you like. It makes no difference in the end what you believe, if it makes you happy.

"Of course, miss."

She smiled, trying to be polite. She never contradicted me, even when I could tell she disagreed. And that nettled me.

After she left, I reached for the discarded book. There was a good deal Mother tolerated, but she abhorred things left lying about.

The pages had flipped, and my eyes happened

across the chapter heading: "The Opening of the Gates of Faerie."

What tosh.

I slammed the book shut.

I decided to wear the new dress to the party. It was black and narrow, with an ornate gold collar that fairly dripped with flashing gems.

I believed that when one is tired of everything and life is entirely lackluster, one should wear a dress that lies about it.

Being an independent woman, I drove myself. The girls with money and a perpetual sneer for the world came in sleek cars driven by chauffeurs. Many of my friends drove together, laughing and veering and having as much fun to and fro as they had at the party itself. Probably what Marge was doing when she hit a patch of ice at far above the legal limit.

But I didn't want the scrutiny of a drive with friends, the few I still had. There had only been a few parties since my sister's death—blurred things I hardly remember, though I went to them all. Condolences were always offered, and I was sick of them. People are altogether shallow and selfish, but for a short while, after someone dies, they get a good smack in the face and behave as if death was catching.

Featherton Square was alive and pulsing with a steady heartbeat when I arrived. Silver and gold light streamed from every window. The garden and grounds were dotted with golden light.

I parked the roadster away from the fray, along the lengthy drive, and walked the rest of the way under the black sky.

The sounds of the party reached even to the quiet road. It was a stark contrast: the black-and-white night against the bright colors ahead, alive and beckoning with mad, reckless abandon.

For a moment it struck me—just for a moment—that perhaps I preferred the night to the reckless light.

But the moment passed. I reached for my skirt, gripped it in the cold fingers that held my clutch, and trudged up towards the blazing house.

The doorway was as full of people as it was of light, the doors flung wide, not to be shut at all that night. People would stream in and out until the night was thin.

I moved into the embrace of the bright light, out of the privacy of the blackness outside.

The scent of perfume, cologne, and champagne

filled the air.

I cut against the flow of the crowd as they moved inward toward the music and dancing, and I found the nearest table, laid out with champagne flutes, cheese, and a dozen bite-sized delicacies.

I snatched up a flute and stood there, watching the streaming people flow in, turning the fragile glass in indifferent fingers.

"Darling, is that you?"

I glanced over as young, flawless Monique De Flores came over. As girls these days go, she isn't so bad. What you see is what you get, and though there may not be much to her, at least she isn't gossiping behind your back. But she went through men like an heiress through dresses.

It wasn't all her fault. I never met a beau of hers I liked—or trusted further than I could throw him.

But she was alone tonight.

Her red lips parted in a bright smile and she threw thin arms around my shoulders, avoiding my full glass. "You look ravishing, Constance."

"You too, as usual."

"Did you just arrive?"

"Only just." I hold out my full flute in explanation.

"And I. It looks like it's going to be a scream."

"Yes, and a horrendous waste of money."

"What, don't you like it?"

"Yes, I do like it," I lied, letting a smile slide up one side of my mouth. "It's not my money."

"Well, if you want me, I'll be just over there." Monique pointed to one of the quieter corners in the ballroom and retreated. We were talk-over-the-table friends, nothing more. I wasn't going to come find her for the rest of the night, and she knew it.

I stood twirling my untouched champagne gently in my fingers, watching everyone with indifference.

It was a mistake, coming. I felt no more alive than I had before. The music dulled in my ears, the laughter sounded hollow, and the lights faded like an old photograph.

I set down the drink and headed towards the door.

And that's when I saw it.

A black-and-white roadster with curtained windows had pulled up to the front steps. A sudden hush fell over the place like I never have heard before.

The air hummed with anticipation. I assumed it was a singer or a picture star arriving late for the drama of it.

A lean-faced man in a hat and suit got out of the far side of the car and came around to open the door that faced us all.

A small, graceful hand laid itself in his outstretched one and the slim figure of a girl emerged from the automobile, her blonde hair hanging long down her back. She wore a dress of black with hints of silver, and her face, though young, was quiet and a little wonderstruck as she took in the staring crowd.

The room around me caught its breath, and I knew this must be Ella Whittington.

"Give her space," the lean man said, leading her up the stairs on his arm. His face was like a mask, professionally aloof. A gambler's face, I thought.

Ella looked at us all with sweet, glowing eyes. And then she smiled, and it was bright and genuine as sunshine.

She passed on by and the crowd swept up after her like the train of her long dress.

I followed the tide back into the rush and noise of the festivities, wondering—one of my clearest thoughts of the night—how long it would take for society to corrupt this girl, their golden child.

She was the darling of the party that night. Though I never sought her out, it was impossible to avoid her.

Everything seemed to revolve around her presence. She came into a room and the lights were brighter. She left, and everything darkened and went stale.

It did not help matters that her brother was still at

large. That was everyone's favorite subject that night, except perhaps the amount of her impending fortune.

The questions rained thick as stars.

It was so vulgar, this curiosity with her and her fortune and her dangerous reprobate brother. But she told the stories again and answered the questions over and over as if it was the first time.

"Was your father very protective of you?"

"Yes." She'd laugh when they said this.

"How was it that you got the fortune, not your brother?"

"Disinherited!" she replied blithely.

"Have you come out to find a husband?" another would ask.

"Are you asking me?"

Laughter.

"When I marry," she told them all, "it will be for love. I have no reason to be induced otherwise."

This went on for hours. They simply basked in her golden presence. If she noticed their infatuation, or was annoyed by it, she did not show it.

It was one of the first things I noticed about her. A girl like that could be a complete nightmare and people would still flock to her.

But that night, she was patient with everyone.

I remembered that.

Two

The folk of Faerie are not all kind, though it is a beautiful, good place. Monsters too lurk at the doorways and entrances, hoping to carry away the unprotected.

—A History of Faerie and the Folk

THE GOLDEN CHILD came to every party that week. There were three of them. All loud, blinding affairs in someone's mansion. I think they were trying to outdo each other, make the strongest impression possible on their new favorite.

It was good for me—or bad, I suppose—as it gave me ample opportunity to drown my sorrows in the din. A roaring party is one of the safest places to be dead inside. No one notices.

It was the week after that I started to see things. Little things at first.

The first was the lean-faced man who never left the Golden Child's side, who I came to learn was the family's—and now her—lawyer.

It was an accident, I think, but we had an encounter at the fourth party, a breezy affair at a seaside mansion with a third of the partygoers coming by boat. The water was littered with laughter and streamers and dancing light.

I was going down the stairs towards the ballroom, a half-full glass in my hand, when a hard shoulder slammed into me, knocking me down against the rail. The glass fell from my fingers and shattered on the stair, and the strap of my shoe broke, sending the poor thing tumbling down the stairs.

I do not know if it was the lawyer who crashed into me or another rowdy partygoer—I am inclined to think the latter, as the entire staircase was crammed with people, but the lawyer was suddenly standing over me. Oddly, the others didn't touch him. He was entirely unruffled. Not a hair out of place.

"Miss." He held out his hand to help me up.

"Thank you," I replied out of habit, and grasped it.

He lifted me to my feet with ease. There was glass all around me.

"With your permission—"

He reached down and scooped me up in his arms, heading down the stairs, over the glass, down towards the prodigal shoe. The glass ground horribly under his shoes.

Past all danger, he set me on my feet. He felt too lean and too strong for a lawyer, a man who sits all day at a desk.

"You're not injured?" He adjusted his glasses and looked at me through them with eyes the color of a frozen pond. There was something vague and almost inhuman in the way they assessed my face, as if I was an inheritance law to be stretched or found a way around.

"No, I am all right," I replied, holding my ground, though I quite wanted to step back from him.

"Good." He smiled blandly and resumed his progress up the stairs.

I gave no thought to the fact at the time, but he was headed in the wrong direction, away from the room where the Golden Child was currently holding court, towards the room where the rich young men smoked and bragged and placed bets on horses and cards. It was one of the few times I ever saw him away from her side.

. . .

The second incident was of a different sort.

Truly, it amazes me how many of the people deemed successes spend their time in this manner. The men making the laws? Smoking in clouds so thick you can't see them. The most beautiful women in all the land? Abusing their bodies to preserve their beauty. The heroes? Drinking away the memories of those days in the gardens.

That is why the Shabby Lord stood out.

That was not his name, of course. It was something long and respectable—Colonel Edward Dennis Abernathy Streatfield or something of the like. He was a war hero, the last dusty allowance of the old guard. His views were decidedly not in vogue, but no one really bothered him because of his service. He was decorated in multiple countries for his contributions to a very large war once, but he was always here now, and his money—people said—sat and collected dust.

As you shall see, people were not entirely correct on that point.

He was invited to every party, despite the fact that his entire being was set against this type of life. Sober-minded, taking no more than a single glass of wine, and inclined to talk of politics in an earnest way that indicated he actually cared—he was altogether a strange sort of relic, and the ladies of my acquaintance loved to poke fun at him in the privacy of our own circles. After all, he did not seek out the popular set as a rule.

Until the night of the Ashton party. I saw him in the same old corner he always found at parties—close to the cigar smokers, but not quite so close as to ruin his jacket —and lo and behold! he picked up his single glass of the night and wound his way towards the Golden Child and her massive court of admirers.

He cut straight through them with his quiet military efficiency and walked right up to her.

"Good evening." He cleared his throat. "You must be Ella Whittington."

"And you must be Colonel Streatfield!" She sprang from her seat, sounding as if she had been waiting her whole life to meet him. The crowd around her murmured a little, uncomfortable at his presence—and quite a presence it was, for the man had the aspect of a willow tree.

"I am." He shifted his feet slightly and gave her a crisp, polite bow.

"You were a war hero. There's even a line about you in my history book."

The Shabby Lord made a dismissive gesture. "The history books are hardly the place for living men."

"I think it suits you," she replied warmly. "Anyhow,

Father had nothing to say against you, and he had a good deal to say against nearly everyone."

"I knew both your father and your brother well," said the colonel kindly. "It was a pity that they had to part on ill terms."

A faint shadow fell over Ella's face and she nodded.

"Did you know your brother well?"

"Only through letters."

"He could make the sea appear in a teacup, stars in a dark room. Your brother had the blessings of the faeries in his hands. You have them in your smile."

"Colonel Streatfield," she said, reaching out and taking his hand in both of hers, "that is the loveliest thing anyone has ever said to me."

"Your brother is a fine man, Miss Ella. I am happy to see you are cut from the same cloth."

"I am so very glad to hear it. I only ever saw him on stage—Father never permitted me to visit him."

"More's the pity. He has a good heart."

"You don't believe, then, that he killed my father?" Ella asked softly.

"Impossible," replied Streatfield. "He is the last man I know who'd kill another. And for his sake, any blood of his will always be welcome in my home."

"And you in mine."

Behind her, from a respectful distance, her lawyer

cleared his throat.

She gestured to the seats. "Will you join us?"

"I would rather not tonight," replied the colonel, looking at the crowd. "But if you ever want to hear stories of your father or your brother, I will always be at your service."

He left her, and there was a low hum of excitement. It was not popular, this praising of Sydney Whittington. A fugitive, a murderer, a strange magician, not to mention the stories about his family—there seemed no end to the strikes against him.

"You've seen your brother on stage?" asked one young man, an heir to a fortune who lived like it.

"Yes, a few times."

"Which of his acts did you enjoy?" asked Monique, twirling the end of her hair in her long fingers.

"I loved his Mastery of Flame. And his Stars of the Heavens. I don't know how he could bring flame from nothing at all. And the stars—you could almost reach out and touch them. I wanted to see that act again and again, but Father never permitted me to see an act more than once. He said it ruined the purity."

There was a mixed response to this.

"Your brother had his flaws, but he was a showman through and through," declared a hearty sportsman-type with a mustache. "No one did it better."

"You don't know where he is, do you?" asked a young woman in a scandalous tone. "I hear your home is full of secret rooms and strange doorways."

Ella laughed kindly. "I assure you, I am as much in the dark as all of you. This is the home I have grown up in, and Sydney has not been through the doors more than a few times since I was born."

"Do you feel afraid of him? That he'll steal the inheritance back?"

"Oh, no," Ella laughed. "He's been written out completely."

"So you are in no danger?" pressed another.

"None at all. I assume he's fled abroad. If anything were to happen to me, the money would simply go to a distant relative, under the supervision of my lawyer."

For an instant, the attention of the room went to the silent man against the wall, his hands folded judiciously, but it returned to their golden child the next moment, and the questions continued, leaving the subject of Sydney behind.

And then I saw the strangest thing, the third of the little things I noticed: the police investigator, Albert Rothschild, standing on the edge of the crowd, a delicate glass in his strong fingers, his eyes roaming subtly over the crowd.

Three

Another of the dangers is faerie-beasts. They do not live in Faerie—they have been cast out and often prowl the doorways, hoping to get back in. But do not be fooled. Beasts do not all have claws and sharp teeth. Some look very ordinary indeed.

—A History of Faerie and the Folk

I REMEMBER, of course, the day Leone showed up. I know it was his first entrance because there was a visible stir when he came. If he had been seen before by even one of the young heiresses in my circle, they would all have known about him already.

He had wicked, beautiful hazel-green eyes.

Leone was handsome, boyishly handsome, but tall and strong like a man. His eyes missed nothing, his smile flashed like camera bulbs to everyone, his gaze lingered on the richest, most extravagant things. And I knew, in my bored, impersonal state of mind, that trouble had just walked in the door.

He had Monique on his arm and she was glowing. Every inch of her lean face was radiant, sharp with joy.

Of course they'd found each other.

A crowd was forming around them, nearly as thick as the one that had flocked around Ella on her first night. But Leone did not seem bothered by the attention. He was basking in it.

Monique, even in her enviable position, had a precarious seat. A dozen girls would be aiming to take him from her in the next hour, and he seemed the sort of man who could be stolen.

"Darling!" Monique led him to me and took my hand in her thin, graceful fingers. "This is Leone and he is my new beau. He's from down south, where it stays warm all year long."

She laughed and looked at him, her eyes adoring.

"Pleasure," I said, without a hint of pleasure in my voice, and held out my hand. Instead of shaking it, he lifted it in bold fingers and kissed it.

"The pleasure is all mine." A glint came into his eyes and his lips parted in a white charmer's smile.

"Apparently," I replied, unrelenting. He was trying to use his charm on me, and I wouldn't have it. I did not like being taken in.

"Monique has told me about you. Only good."

"Then she has hardly been truthful."

"That's all right," he replied, twining his fingers back over Monique's. "I like my friends wild."

I smiled at him, a little bitterly. Sure enough, trouble had walked in the door. When he turned his back, I shot Monique a look. But she only smiled blissfully at me and put her arm through his.

As she let him away through the crowd, he looked back over his shoulder and winked at me.

They cut a wide, blazing swath through the crowd of young hopefuls. And I stayed where I was. I had no desire to be near that man.

They were replaced by the glum but professional presence of Inspector Rothschild.

He was properly known as the head police investigator, but in my mind I called him the Wolf-Catcher. He was little better than that, put on the case of the escaped Sydney Whittington, who—if the gossip was true—had left the force precisely no leads.

It appeared the inspector's task was to shadow Ella

Whittington's public appearances (a desperate attempt, in my opinion), but this required him to listen to more gossip than is healthy and hold champagne as if he actually meant to drink it, and to a man like him...well, he already appeared to have had his full of our kind.

He looked sad and weary, in a wry sort of way.

"Evening." He raised his eyebrows at me and downed his champagne with a flat expression.

"Work or pleasure?" I dropped my pearls. I'd been absently fingering them, counting compulsively.

"Hm." His laugh was brief and dry.

"Salut." I clinked my glass against his. "May you find what you're looking for. Though, I must say, isn't following Ella a bit of a desperate chance?"

"They were known to correspond. Miss Whittington is entirely innocent, I can tell you that. Very nice girl."

He gave me a thin smile and moved on.

He drifted, poor man, for the rest of the night around the drink tables and the dance floors, and though he disappeared at times, I always saw him reappear like a melancholy apparition from the back halls.

Finally, someone who looked as miserable as I was. Everyone else, with their laughter and their gossip—they couldn't understand the hopelessness of it all.

I wandered down nearer to the dancing. At a party

like this, the restless young men flocked together, and I could always find one who wanted to dance. When you are moving fast, when the music whirls in your ears and you are the center of a man's world for three minutes, it's harder to think. And I was tired of thinking just then.

I danced for a while, just long enough to be flushed and laughing too hard. I was abandoned by my partner for a loud blonde, and that's when I saw that Ella had come down to the dance floor.

Monique and Leone, who were both incredible dancers, had been dancing longer than I had, and they were just to my left when I saw Leone turn his head—and he saw Ella too.

He froze like he'd seen an angel.

Just then, the music turned to something brisk and driving, quick and clean as the shifting of gears in an automobile.

Leone kissed Monique's hand gallantly and turned around, his eyes fixed on Ella as she stood on the fringe of the crowd, watching the musicians with interest.

He moved across the floor towards her, clapping in time with the music, his mouth quirked to one side in his roguish smile.

The music rose and rose, demanding a response. The floor was filling behind him like the tide rushing in, and still he pressed on toward her, those hazel-green eyes sparkling.

Don't do it, girl. Turn around and run the other way.

Her expression turned from one of interest to puzzlement, and then surprise as he reached out and took her hand.

He didn't ask, he didn't even try to posture. Just took her hand and drew her into the wild music with him. It was too bold and probably what every other young man had wanted to do for the last week.

The lawyer didn't even have time to react. Leone swept her away into the music, and they were gone.

By the time I caught another glimpse, they were in the center of the floor and he was twirling her as if they were the only two people in the world.

Her face was flushed and surprised, but she could have stepped off that floor any moment she wanted, and she didn't. She matched him step for step.

Everyone else was mesmerized. I was too, for a few moments at least. Her hair spun like golden silk in the bright lights, and her face, usually polite and cheerful, was radiant. Leone's face was still a charming mask, but there was a wild glint in his eyes, like he'd tear apart anyone who tried to take her from him.

Trouble was coming, I knew it then.

The song ended. The two of them were caught on the floor, still entranced, for the space of a heartbeat.

And then with a smile, bold and brighter than the lights overhead, Leone led the way off the floor.

"Thank you for the dance," he said. "What is your name?"

She looked up at him quizzically, but there was a kind of adoration beginning in her eyes.

"Ella. Whittington."

"Leone. Utterly charmed."

He went back to Monique, who also looked puzzled, but for different reasons. But he kissed her hand and smiled at her, and she was not angry. After that display, everyone wanted him all the more.

Except for me, of course.

I know what trouble looks like, no matter what form it takes.

Leone ran into me at the tables later that evening, almost as if he'd been looking for me.

"Excuse me." He paused, mischief appearing on his face. "I didn't catch your name earlier."

"Would you have remembered even if I'd told you?" I asked, setting aside my glass.

He took a step closer to me, a sparkle coming into his

eye even as his charmer's smile started up one sharp corner of his mouth. "Yours, I would."

"Then I won't tell you." I returned the smile coolly. "You don't need more names."

"I stand rebuked," he smiled, looking not remotely rebuked.

"Enjoy your night," I replied ironically, and turned my back.

I don't know what he thought of that, but I'd learned the best way to communicate with an over-friendly young man at a party was not with subtlety. Subtlety should be saved for gardens and sitting rooms and dinner conversation.

I don't know what he did with himself the rest of the evening. But I did see him again with Monique later, talking quietly in a corner, their faces grave and genuine, and against every instinct I had, I wished them well in my heart.

Four

❧

At the change of every season, the Queen chooses a new crown: of snowdrops, of daisies, of falling leaves—and in the winter, of flakes from the first snowfall of the season.

—A History of Faerie and the Folk

I WOKE up very late the next morning. The summer sun was streaming lazily through the bedroom windows, filtered gently through the white linen curtains. The night before felt like a distant, vaguely soured dream.

I could hear the bustle of someone preparing to leave; at this hour, it would certainly be mother and not father.

Sure enough, her voice came floating up the stairwell a minute later.

"Constance, I am taking fresh flowers down to the cemetery. Would you like to come?"

"No, mother," I called down, glad I hadn't dressed yet.

I took down a light chiffon morning gown and laid it out on the bed. At least with mother gone, the house would be quiet. I'd take tea in the garden and read a book—or pretend to. I didn't read much, but I felt more useful having a book nearby.

"Constance."

I turned around to face my mother in her silks and hat, framed in the doorway.

"You haven't gone to the cemetery once since the funeral," she declared, her face set for a fight. "It's only right that you take a week, same as your father and I."

"Marge and I were not chums," I retorted. "I am not going to pretend we were now that she's gone."

My mother drew herself up like an offended black swan.

"Constance Hanover, you will do your duty by your family."

"I am not a child, mother," I answered her, rather childishly. "And I am not dressed, anyway. Some other time."

"I do not like you going to these parties, being out late. You are not in a state to be taxing yourself that way."

"And what state am I in?"

"Your sister has been dead only three months. You are not yourself."

"Since when did Marge have any effect on my life?"

She fixed me with a stern look. "All that aside, there is something up this season, and I don't like you constantly out in company."

She left, mercifully cutting off the argument. I wasn't about to stop going, and I wasn't about to go out in black silks to lay flowers every third week for the world to see. Anyone who knew us knew how Marge and I got on, which was hardly at all. And I didn't want anyone speculating that I'd had a change of heart just because her foolish, reckless living caught up to her.

I shut my bedroom door, muffling the sounds of my mother's departure, and changed into my morning dress.

The dance from the night before kept playing in my head like a beautiful nightmare I could not part from. I wasn't sure if I was attracted or repulsed.

I was moved, however. I felt something. And that was unusual.

The rest of the day, I lounged about. I was in a sour mood after arguing with my mother, and while the parties did not make me happy, the lack of stimulation afterwards always bordered on unbearable.

The only thing notable about that day was that the dance, fleeting and strange as it was, remained in the back of my mind, as something. Something that I felt, with growing conviction, was the beginning of something important.

At the next party, Leone arrived fashionably late with Monique on his arm. She was in a glittering silver dress, but her face outshone that dress. Leone had a smile for every person he passed, especially the ladies, but his arm remained firmly in Monique's.

They stopped by the food, sampling it, laughing—Leone pointed out delicacies and teased Monique about them, and she was more than happy to be teased. It was the one and only time I saw them look happy together. There was an easy gentleness in his manner toward her, and she beamed under the attention. Leone served himself a glass of punch and handed Monique a champagne, and they went over to the place where Ella held court.

The crowd around Ella was always frightful, but still, I found with great consistency, it was the brightest and happiest place at any gathering.

Still holding Monique's hand, Leone cut through the crowd with the ease of a knife through silk until he had penetrated the innermost circle and stood before the Golden Child herself.

"Miss Whittington, is it always so hard to get near you?" he asked, as he urged a young man out of his seat and sat down near her.

"You had less trouble than most," she replied quietly and turned her gaze to Monique. "You are Monique De Flores, aren't you?"

"Yes." She smiled and held out a manicured hand.

"It's a pleasure." Ella took her hand, and there was no affectation in the gesture, just the genuine pleasure she professed.

"Has anyone brought you a drink?" asked Leone.

"No, I don't drink," Ella answered. "At least, not what you have."

There was a titter at Leone's expense, likely from the sort who hoped he would notice them by their reaction. Which he did not; his eyes were fixed on Ella.

"A tonic, then?" he pressed.

"Not right now." She smiled kindly to spare him embarrassment, but she did not seem entirely comfortable with his boldness.

I could not shake the memory of how easily she had danced with him, how she had nearly floated over the ground as he spun her. There was certainly more to it than the music. Perhaps it was the kind of magic that followed her around; everything she touched turned to gold.

"As you like." Leone leaned back in his newly-stolen chair and hooked one long knee over the other. "I don't suppose, at your age, you have ever been abroad?"

"No," she admitted. "I want to go, but my lawyer thinks it isn't wise until I have received my inheritance." She glanced back at the figure against the wall.

"And your lawyer is permitted to make these decisions? For shame. You are the heiress! You must go abroad, I insist."

"It isn't that simple." Ella touched the necklace at her throat and shook her head. "He says there are many things to consider. But—I do think a little time abroad in the winter could hardly hurt."

"For you, it would be your making. I am sure of it."

"My making?" This seemed to catch her attention.

"You haven't seen beauty until you have seen the sun set over the mountains or stood along the edge of a canal under the gleam of the city lights. More than that, they will not have understood beauty themselves until they've seen your face, lit up with joy."

His eyes were gleaming—cherishing—and his voice was gentle.

And Ella, love-starved and alone as she was, saw it.

Something changed in her from that moment on, I am certain. In her position, who would not have been touched?

"That is quite a thing to say," she ventured, confusion standing between her eyes.

"It costs me no effort. None at all."

Monique sat watching, the color stronger than usual in her beautiful face, but there was no anger in her expression, no effort to stop this change. Ella's lawyer watched too, from his place against the wall, but if he was disturbed, he said nothing. We all watched, all the same: mere players in their story, unwilling and unable to exert ourselves to change anything.

"You should...." Ella hesitated, searching for words. "You should not drink so much punch."

"I haven't touched the punch," Leone replied quietly. "Not a drop." He lifted his full cup and passed it on to a young woman who seemed more than happy to be the subject of his attention for two seconds.

"No, it is something altogether more wonderful that draws me here—that draws us all here." He gestured to the substantial crowd. "We have all come to bask in your golden light."

Ella laughed at this, a strong, genuine laugh. She didn't know what she was, which was exactly what made her wonderful. She didn't believe a word of his flattery.

"Your brother called himself a magician," said Leone, "but you are the real magician."

"Now, that's not true," said Ella, shaking her head. "Didn't you ever see him perform?"

"Can't say as I did." Leone smiled wickedly. "Can't say as I'd have wanted to. Sounds like a proper stuffed shirt."

"You can't go saying things like that about my family."

"Even after all the scandal?"

"I don't believe he did what they accuse him of," said Ella, the conviction in her voice rising. "Before long it'll be cleared up, and we will be able to meet properly. I have always wanted to meet him, and Father wouldn't allow it."

"That is very unlikely," interjected her lawyer. "When they catch him, he is sure to be hanged."

Ella turned around in her chair.

"Mr. Simmonds, why must you always be talking of hanging? He's not been proven guilty, and having a row with Father does not make him a murderer."

"And yet his name was on the arrest warrant," the lawyer supplied coolly.

Ella turned away from him, forcing a pleasant

expression back onto her face. "Well, I suppose we've exhausted that topic."

The conviction in her voice and manner only seemed to have attracted Leone further. As the talk continued he leaned forward, a sparkle in his eyes, drawn in like a moth to flame.

I watched as the minutes went by, watched as Leone slipped further and further from Monique, who just sat in silence, letting it happen.

I was in my own sort of mood. After a short while, I left the Golden Child's court for the dubious pleasures of drifting around the tables and the dusty corners where the politicians lurked.

I was surprised, though perhaps I shouldn't have been, when Monique turned up at my elbow, fresh champagne in her hand.

"What is this? What happened to Leone?"

"He's just in the other room." She gave a dismissive wave. "I am tired tonight."

"Are you going early?"

"Only if Leone goes. I know better than to leave him in the hands of the others."

Another reason I did not want a beau. It was sad how quickly people could run from person to person, toying with hearts and smashing feelings like china dolls.

Still, having a beau was exciting. It was a rush, like speeding in your automobile. It made life seem more real and everything around you far more wonderful.

It was a gamble, I suppose.

"May I tell you something, Constance? I don't care if it is scandalous." Monique tossed her head, suddenly determined.

"Say it."

"I just want to be loved. That's it. Forget the new automobiles, the pearls, the expensive wine, everything. I want someone to look at me when I wake up in the morning with the same look he'd give me walking into a party in an evening gown, just because of who I was. But that—that is harder to find than a rich heir."

She took a weary sip of her champagne.

"You don't think Leone will love you like that?" I asked. I had my own opinions on it, but her confession was an honest one and I wanted to know where her mind was.

"He's happy to stay with me for now, while he's passing through," said Monique with a shrug. "It's better than having no one." She toyed with the tips of her gloved fingers. "And you never know, I suppose. A girl can have her dreams."

I agreed that a girl could. But I knew better than to dream myself. Dreams were things that broke and cut your fingers when they did.

We walked back to the room together, but I had no intention of staying.

"Monique!" Ella greeted her as we walked in. She came over to us, bringing the golden light with her, leaving her place at the front of the room cold and empty.

But after a brief nod to Monique, she turned to me.

"What is your name?"

"Constance."

"Constance. I am Ella." She held out her hand, introducing herself with no pretension, giving her name as if she assumed everyone didn't know it. "I see you at every party and I always see you alone. You are welcome to come sit with me whenever you like."

My customary protest rose to my lips. I was in no mood to be part of this. But it died when I looked her in the face to speak. Her face was kind and eager.

"Thank you," was all that came out of my lips, too used to irony and bitter words.

I followed her light back to the center of attention, and one of her usual admirers moved, without a word, to give me a seat of honor.

"Make yourself comfortable." Ella sat down and

folded her hands in her lap, fixing me with an earnest look.

Leone was across from me, watching me with a faint sparkle in his eye, but I pointedly ignored him. Sitting here in the inner circle where all the attention was fixed was hardly comfortable, and I was taking a keener dislike to Leone with every passing minute.

"You live at Hanover Square, don't you?" asked Ella. "It's a beautiful estate."

"Yes. How did you know?"

"I remember seeing you once, when my father visited yours. You were heading out."

"I see." I have no recollection, and I hope I didn't say anything rude. If our fathers were visiting each other, Ella would have been young indeed, and I at the age where company more than a year or two younger was intolerable.

"Hanover Square. Lovely gardens, right?" Leone crooked an eyebrow.

"Yes." I didn't like how much he seemed to know.

"You love gardens, don't you, Ella? Flowers and all?"

The talk swung towards flowers and away from me, because Leone could change the flow of conversation like water in a canal.

And I thought, mistakenly, that that was the end of that.

Five

The people of Faerie are bright and kind and merry.
They are fond of late-night dances, bright stars, and the
light of the moon.

—A History of Faerie and the Folk

Two DAYS LATER, Regina met me in the front hall as I came in from a morning's jaunt to town.

"Miss Hanover, an invitation came to you, direct with instructions to wait for your reply."

"A reply?" I had no idea what sort of invitation this could be. "Where is the invitation?"

The maid went over to the front table and brought it over.

It was small stationary, not the ostentatious kind of thing that usually accompanied such requests.

I tore it open with the letter opener we kept on the table and pulled out the small missive. It was neat, modest handwriting.

Miss Hanover,

I should be honored to have you to tea on Tuesday the third, at three o'clock. Please do come. I await your response.

Your obedient servant,

Miss Ella Whittington.

I turned the letter round once, looking for a hint that perhaps it was merely a joke, but there was no such indication.

"Where is the messenger?"

"In the kitchen."

"Have him come."

With the maid sent away, I went to my writing desk and took out a clean sheet. My intention had been to write my regrets, but somewhere between dipping the pen and putting it to paper, the words *"Thank you, I should be honored to accept your gracious invitation"* came forth and I further ensnared myself by signing my name *Constance* below.

He left with the reply, and I went upstairs to pick out a dress to play tennis.

It was an aggressively sunny day, Tuesday the third—the sort that is so intent on its sunniness that you rather suspect foul play, and somewhere in the late afternoon your best plans are likely to be ruined by a veritable clapper of a thunderstorm.

I drove myself over in my roadster and pulled up to the very large gates, which stood bound. I'd never had any reason to go to the Whittington place, but it had always held an ancient aura of mystery and foreboding and things you couldn't understand, things that never quite mixed with the new shine of parties and wild living.

I climbed out of the car and went over to the gate-keeper's booth. It was an old place, and I didn't know if they even had a gatekeeper.

A stern-faced man checked my invitation and waved me in without a word.

I pulled into the spacious drive and ground to a halt

on the old paving stones of the driveway. The house was enormous and beautiful and looked as if it had already stood two hundred years and would stand two hundred more. It must have been something wonderful in the days when it held parties and laughter instead of jealousy and murder.

I left the automobile to the attendant and made for the set of doors he indicated.

I knocked, then rang the bell, and a servant came and opened it for me.

Ella was waiting just beyond, and she came up and clasped my hand. "I am so happy to see you."

She greeted me as if I was an old friend she was dying to see, but even here, in the safety of her home, I could find no trace of insincerity.

She was truly happy to see me. I suppose I should have expected it by now.

"Tea will be in the garden," she said. "It's a beautiful day for it."

"It is," I agreed, still a bit puzzled by the warm welcome.

"This way."

She led me out into an immaculately kept garden, in the center of which, under a gazebo, stood a table full of tea sandwiches, cakes, and fruits.

I don't think I said much of anything as we walked

out; I was taking in the wide gardens and the quiet, rich atmosphere of the place.

Ella settled herself, smoothing her skirt before reaching for the piping hot teapot. She poured first into my cup and then into hers.

"You seem to be the only person who is not eager to make my acquaintance."

"Mm." I glanced up, and her eyes met mine.

"I hope I've done nothing to offend you," she said quietly. Then her eyes twinkled a little. "After all, everyone is eager to make my acquaintance—or my money's, rather."

"That's true," I admitted, a little impressed that she should assess the situation so accurately. Perhaps her lawyer had told her as much. "I have nothing against you personally, I simply hate the mania over money."

"I am glad to hear that." Her face lit up. "I think perhaps we will be friends, then."

Normally I would have said something dry and off-putting, but to her, I merely smiled. A person would be a fool to turn away such a genuine smile.

"Is that why you have brought me here? For a personal interview?"

"No, nothing so scheming. I am lonely—in this big house, in the company of so many other people—and you, at least, have not tried to flatter me."

"You have hit upon my one good quality," I replied wryly. "I am afraid I have no more."

"Everyone has more than one, I am convinced of that."

"Well, I wish you luck finding it, because I do not know what it is."

Ella looked at me with surprise and burst into delighted laughter.

"Constance, I think you enjoy being cynical."

"Cynicism is just reality."

"I am not sure about that," Ella replied, sipping her tea thoughtfully. "I think some of the most beautiful things in this world are also the truest."

I didn't agree, but I wasn't about to start a disagreement. So I shrugged, pasted on an agreeable smile, and served myself a tea sandwich.

"Monique told me your sister died earlier this year." Ella looked up at me suddenly. "I am sorry."

"Don't be," I answered quickly. "We were not close."

Ella nodded quietly. "I wasn't close with my father. And he did not allow me to be close to anyone else, really."

"You seem so happy despite it."

"I had a good governess," said Ella with a little smile. "We read books and poetry for hours."

"Where is she now that you're out?"

"Oh, Father dismissed her six months ago. I was getting too old, anyway."

Ella poured herself a fresh cup and took her time with the milk and sugar before she continued.

"My father was not always kind, but I do miss him. I find it strange that though a person can be unkind or cruel, still, if they are family, your feelings for them are mixed with affection or longing."

I took a sip of my tea and said nothing. Marge had been shallow and selfish. I couldn't feel any longing for her, only deep annoyance and anger at her for dying and cementing herself as something to be remembered fondly.

If Ella thought I should agree with her about my own experience, she didn't show it. Her face was open and a little sad as she sipped her tea and looked out over the garden.

There was an angry little knot of blue over the far trees.

"What do you think of Leone?"

"Leone?" I choked on my tea.

"Yes." Her expression was shadowed with a small frown between her eyes.

"Well...." I composed myself, recovering from the tea. "He is very charming."

"But you are not charmed by him."

"I am not charmed by anyone."

"He seems fond of me," she ventured. "But he is Monique's beau. I'm not fond of him in that way, I'm not—but it puzzles me."

"You can send him packing, you know."

"I don't want to be unkind after he's been nothing but kind."

"Kind for the sake of your money, mark my words."

"It's something deeper," she persisted. "In his eyes."

"Love?" I supplied dryly.

"I don't know." Ella bit her knuckle thoughtfully. "I have seen men in love and I don't think it's that. He's not quite like the others."

"If you think that, then you're already falling," I replied. "He's just bolder, is all. He takes before he asks."

"Is it wrong to entertain him?"

"You're asking me?" I touched my hand to my chest in surprise.

"Well—yes."

"I don't advise against anything that makes people happy," I said, neatly sidestepping the direct question. "Happiness doesn't last, so one may as well snatch it up before it goes stale."

"But the best things don't come quickly," supplied

Ella. "I know that. Cheap goods always wear out the fastest."

"Then send him packing. Unless you're sure he loves you, and I mean you and not your money, send him away. He'll only break your heart."

A grumble came from the sky, close, and a breeze rustled the trees, flowing over us and raising the edge of the tablecloth.

Ella just cut herself a piece of cake and took a pensive bite.

"If you don't mind my asking," I said, leaning forward a little, "do you ever wish you didn't have the inheritance, the attention, all the eyes of society on you?"

"Of course." She laughed, clear and refreshing. Guileless. "But it's what I've been given. There's no sense in moaning about it."

"I suppose not."

"But I do wish to settle some of it on my brother, if he is exonerated." She lowered her voice as she said this. "My lawyer is set against it. He said it would be directly against my father's wishes and that the will wouldn't allow it. I wish—"

Rain broke out around us, pelting the gazebo roof and whisking in on the rushing wind.

"Oh—oh dear, the cake!" Ella laughed, rushing to

cover it.

I stood up, looking around for a way of escape, which there wasn't. I knew the beautiful day had been too good to be true.

But there was something else inside me, something that felt uneasy about that moment. Before it started raining. I couldn't put my finger on it. Perhaps it was that she seemed about to break off what she was going to say even before the rain broke out.

"What are we going to do?" I asked, with an exasperated laugh.

"Someone will be coming out for us soon." Ella peered through the curtain of rain. "I would make a dash for it if I thought it was wise."

"Is it not?" I looked over at her with a dry smile.

Her eyes danced with fun. "I will if you will."

"Miss Ella, Miss Hanover!" one of the staff shouted through the rain, coming towards us on long, mud-spattered legs, followed by a small regiment of umbrellas. "Are you all right?"

Ella shot me a slightly disappointed look. "Yes, we are just staying dry!" she called back.

"Good." He gained the gazebo and stepped up into its safety. "We will take you inside. Would you like a fresh pot of tea?"

"Yes, please. We are damp," replied Ella, gathering

her skirt in her hands and stepping down under an offered umbrella. "And bring the cake, if it survives."

We were put up in the library instead, where a good fire was started, changing the air and aspect of the day entirely.

The teacup cradled in my hands made it feel like Christmas, not summer, and the rain pounded the glass panes of the second story window.

I had been advised by the staff not to go home until it abated, lest a wayward tree fall upon the road and strand me, and while I thought that a rather silly concern, I had agreed and phoned to leave a message for my mother, lest she worry.

It used to be of no concern where we went and how we used our time, but after Marge, she worries.

There, again, Marge's wildness was coming back to ruin my life, not hers.

"What a great number of books you have," I commented, looking at the walls covered floor to ceiling.

"Yes—they were collected by my grandfather."

"Do you read them?"

"Sometimes." Ella fingered the end of her long golden hair, studying the ends. "The library was a favorite haunt of my brother's, so my father didn't like to be in here and he didn't like me in here either."

"I see."

"My grandfather collected books on the mysteries of Faerie. He was convinced he'd been there when he was a little boy. That's why everyone said he was mad."

"Did you know him?"

"No. He died when I was a week old. But he got to hold me, I hear."

The door opened, and Ella's lawyer thrust his head in.

"Excuse me."

He came in, giving Ella and I a slight nod and going over to the bookshelf. He pulled down a couple volumes before retreating out the open door and back down the long corridor.

"Is your lawyer always about the place?" I asked, following the man with my eyes.

"Yes. He has a house in Clearside and an office in Brookshire, but he is always here first thing in the morning, and he is often in the study long after I am asleep. He is a—a very hard worker."

"What is there to manage here?"

"Everything, I suppose. My father was his only client. There are account books to check, correspondence to write, the banks to keep informed, the inheritance law to go over. He says it is dreadfully complicated and I should be bored to hear it all."

"Are you?"

"Not as bored as he imagines. But it is dull," she laughed.

"He is a strange man," I commented, not even knowing why I said it.

"Yes—" Ella agreed, looking away at that moment to pull at a loose thread on her chair. She didn't continue.

It has been said that in the world, there are mortals with faerie hearts. These are people who see beauty in everything, and goodness as greater than power.

—A History of Faerie and the Folk

THE NEXT DAY, Leone appeared at a party with Ella on his arm. I was surprised, after all the doubts she had voiced the day before, but there they were, together, with Monique nowhere in sight.

I saw Monique two days later at a friend's house, where I was playing tennis with a group.

We had taken a break for sandwiches and lemonade,

and we were short a glass, so I'd put down my racket and gone inside to look for one.

And there was Monique, sitting in a chair, lovelorn and listless.

A lit cigarette rested in her fingers, but she was not smoking it. The smoke just wound lazily upward as she rested her chin on the narrow arm she had draped over the back of the chair. Her entire manner was that of a girl who'd just been jilted.

"I didn't see you up at the Dells'," I said.

"Mhm. I didn't go." She didn't pick her head up or move at all.

"Do you—want to talk about it? He is a rake."

"No, he isn't." Monique turned around, lolling her head back against the chair.

"He jilted you."

"Yes," she replied languidly. "But you know what, darling? The right thing is so much better than the easy thing."

She lifted the cigarette to her lips and drew on it once before snuffing it out.

I didn't know what she meant then.

Monique came alone to the next party, one held by Senator Armentrout, who was no doubt looking to ingratiate himself with people before the next election.

I think she noticed me when she came in, but an hour or more passed and she made no effort to find me.

Inspector Rothschild was there, looking weary as usual, his untouched glass in his hand, making a show of blending in but keeping his wits sharp.

Then I saw Hector Marion walk in—a wealthy young man, freshly back from abroad, and an old flame of mine. It had taken me all of two evening parties to know I hadn't a shred of respect for him, and thankfully, he found me altogether too dry and boring.

Even so, I was not in the mood for an encounter, so I headed for the nearest exit.

Outside, the night sounds were dimmed and the laughter softened. It was as if a blanket had been thrown over the noise and wildness, and for a moment, it almost felt like relief.

And that was when I met the Serious One.

I first noticed him in the garden beside the nasturtiums, a tall, still figure standing outside the reach of the gaudy lights. At first I thought to ignore him. Everyone else clearly had.

But something drew me to him. Perhaps it was the set of his shoulders or the solemn way he regarded the lights; I am not sure. I set down my champagne on the nearest garden table and made my way over.

He noticed me coming and raised his eyebrows, but he did not move. As I stepped into the shadow, I saw that he was dressed smartly, his brown hair combed back, and leaning on a cane. But he was young—my age, perhaps.

"Good evening." He eyed me slowly, as if he wasn't used to people coming over to talk to him.

"Are you new in town? I've never seen you before."

"I'm the senator's son," he supplied briefly, with a small, rueful smile.

"So this is your home."

"Mhm."

"You don't seem happy about the intrusion."

Again, the rueful smile. "My father does what he likes. I do not make a habit of crossing him. There are more important things to bother about."

"Important things?" I laughed. "More important than all that noise and recklessness and forgetting pain?"

"You don't forget your pain," he said softly. His brown eyes met mine and they were honest. "But I agree with you. It is reckless. It's a waste."

"Don't tell me you never enjoy this?"

"I usually decline invitations," he replied. "It's hard for me to leave the house." He shifted the head of his cane in explanation.

"Perhaps it's rude of me to ask, but does it hurt?"

He ground the tip of his cane into the crushed-shell walkway. "It comes and goes. It's all right, I am used to it."

"I see." I realized he was looking at me kindly, almost sympathetically.

"Nicholas Armentrout," he greeted, switching his cane to his left hand and holding out his right.

"Constance Hanover."

"I was sorry to hear about your sister."

"You knew Marge?"

"Only of her, sadly."

"You didn't miss much," I replied.

A strange look passed over his face but he said nothing.

He nodded instead towards the house, lit up to the eaves."Do you know what this reminds me of?" He twisted the end of his cane into the patch of dirt beside him. "A ship, burning before it sinks. It's the brightest it ever is as it slides into the sea, never to rise. These people are blazing, glorious wrecks, and after a year, no one will remember any of this."

I laughed and answered that I certainly would be one of them.

But I did remember. I remember his words, his face, as clearly as if we were still standing beside the nasturtiums. I knew I was looking at someone deep and tragic and honest. He couldn't have grabbed my attention more if he'd slapped me in the face.

I felt that for a brief moment, some great curtain was pulled back and I had seen reality.

A shout broke out across the garden.

It was Hector Marion, lunging for someone's throat, his voice thick with anger and too much drink.

"I know what you did! What you do when you think no one sees! See if you have the courage to fight me face to face. I'll take you with pistols or fists, just see!"

Monique was silhouetted against the bright windows, clutching her long necklace in tight fingers, watching Hector rave. Every so often, she would voice a protest, but it was no good.

Nicholas cleared his throat and craned his neck to see.

"Is there someone in danger?" I asked.

"Not the lady," said Nicholas slowly. "I think he may just be over the limit tonight."

"It's like him," I said. "I avoid him if I can."

Still, out of curiosity, I went closer.

Hector was shouting at Leone, who had put Ella behind him and was facing him down calmly.

"Go home, you've had too much," he was saying, speaking clearly and firmly.

People were starting to murmur and back out of the

way. I caught "Get the inspector" out of the many tangled words.

"I am not going to fight you," said Leone.

"You're a coward, sir!"

"A coward, perhaps, but a fool, no."

"Are you calling me a fool?" Marion raved.

The Wolf-Catcher came running into the garden, spotting the two of them, he slowed to a walk and approached Hector Marion.

"Sir, you need to go home now," he said, calmly.

"Do you know who I am?" he demanded.

"Hector Marion. You are a very important man, I know, and it is time for you to go home."

That gave him pause; he seemed perplexed now that there was no disrespect at which he could take offense.

"Your automobile has been called for, and your chauffeur is ready for you." Rothschild patted him firmly on the back, as a friend might after a particularly good shot.

"If you say so," mumbled Hector.

He stumbled off with Inspector Rothschild at his elbow, and that was the end of it.

Leone let his breath out slowly and then crossed the pavement to Monique, who was standing alone.

"He doesn't know what he's talking about," he said.

She glanced around at the bystanders, then back to

his face. "I know the truth," she said coolly. "Goodnight."

It was near the end of the night when I wandered into a side room, small and dimly lit. It was the sort of place where the most unexpected people might wander in and get caught, like driftwood in a river inlet. I think I was hoping I might come across the Serious One again.

A low murmur of earnest voices from one corner stopped me.

It was Monique and Leone.

Their manner changed almost immediately. Leone looked guilty, as if he'd been caught in something he shouldn't be doing.

"Good evening, Constance," Monique said smoothly, raising her glass, and she moved past me quickly. "I was just taking my leave."

Leone lingered.

"Is there something you want, Miss Hanover?"

"No. I was looking for someone."

He nodded slowly, his eyes on my face as if trying to divine whether I was telling the truth or not.

He brushed past me, so close that I could smell his sharp cologne.

The greatest hero of Faerie is its prince. Though he is quick and clever, he is brave most of all. If ever one of his own is in danger, he comes to their rescue, and he is the special protector of the queen. Should she find herself in danger, he would defend her with his own life.

—A History of Faerie and the Folk

I SHOULD HAVE KNOWN something was going to happen at the Gouldings' that night. They threw the wildest parties, and never a one passed without some kind of disaster.

My mind was strangely set on going, though I could

not have said why. Even Monique, who could walk into dark clouds and be surprised when it rained, had seemed loath to attend when we discussed it the day before.

"Hector insists on going, but I don't know if I want to," she'd said.

"Are you with him or are you not?"

She shrugged. "Not with him exactly, but–"

"You are with him," I sighed. "At least in his mind."

"But you can hardly hear yourself think at the Gouldings'," she had protested.

"Perfect," I'd replied, unsympathetic to the end.

I wandered out into the crowds that night, letting the laughter and gossip flow over me, numb, heedless like a stone under the flow of a river.

Still, I had the presence of mind to realize that something was not quite right.

First of all, the Wolf-Catcher was conspicuously absent. And the Shabby Lord, who usually had nothing to do with the Gouldings, was in attendance, talking earnestly among the lobbyists, his medal-heavy uniform weighing his shoulders down like a tree bent under snow. Monique, despite her protests about attending, passed me, followed by Hector Marion talking about his automobile. He was definitely keen on her. I hesitated for the barest moment, wondering if I shouldn't go and save her, but he was there and I certainly didn't want to talk to him. So I kept walking.

I wandered to the dance floor, watching the couples blur into the deafening music itself. Everything seemed so hollow and gray. Their smiles were just painted on, their movements meaningless. If you stared at one black-and-white tile on the floor, a dozen couples would pass over it and then be gone, lost in the crowd....

And then a crisp, dark blue pair of shoes crossed it, alone, cutting through the music, the whirling dancers, bringing it all to a halt.

"Adolphus Leone?"

There was a sudden uneasy murmur. People were looking around, unsure, talking amongst themselves.

The crowd had parted, leaving him and Ella alone together, and his roguish smile was fading into a confused, angry look. He let go of Ella's hand and let his arm slide away from her waist.

"Are you Adolphus Leone?" asked the policeman. He was a new man. I hadn't seen him before and a quick glance around proved that if Rothschild was here, he wasn't around.

"Just Leone," Leone corrected. "I don't answer to Adolphus."

"But that is your name?"

"I imagine I am the man you're looking for."

"I have a warrant for your arrest."

"Arrest? Impossible." Ella's voice was soft but in the silence of the room, you could hear it clear as day.

"Arrest?" Leone's eyebrows shot up and he smiled, suddenly rakish. "How delightful. On what charge?"

"Fraud, forgery, and inciting political unrest."

"To unrest, I plead guilty," said Leone, his mischievous gaze sweeping over the crowd, "but I don't give a hang for politics. Rat out my accuser for me and we can settle this here and now."

"I am sorry, Mr. Leone, but I must take you for questioning. It will be better for us all if you don't resist."

"No—" Ella pushed past him, putting herself between Leone and the officer. "This must be a mistake! He's not guilty of any of that. I can vouch for him."

"I am sorry, young lady."

"Please." Tears started into her eyes. "I said I can vouch. I have a lawyer—"

She caught the lawyer's eye where he stood, emotionless, along the wall.

"Come here, Simmonds, please."

He stood his ground and merely shook his head.

"Simmonds, please!"

The officer simply pushed past her, brusque and official, and seized Leone's arm.

"No, please." She turned to the policeman. "Don't take him!"

The policeman brushed her off, a little roughly.

"Easy, man, easy!" Leone's voice broke the impending scuffle. "Ella, Ella." His devil-may-care face turned sober for the barest moment and his eyes met hers. "It's all right."

He held up one hand to the policeman, appeasing, and reached for Ella's hand with the other. He pressed it gently in his fingers and kissed it.

He whispered something and she nodded back, though her face was still afraid.

"All right, officer." He turned around to face the man. "I'll go with you."

He stood unresistant as the officer snapped cuffs on his wrists and led him out through the crowd.

"I'll give a kiss to the first one to put up bail," he joked, winking at the dumbfounded crowd.

Ella stood alone in the middle of the floor, her face white, biting her lip to hold back tears.

The crowd remained silent and stunned until they were gone, and then the spell broke. They rushed to Ella, crowding around her.

I almost walked away, as she had more than enough

sympathy—but I glimpsed her face, still white, still lost, and something strange rose in me that I hadn't felt in years.

I strode towards her, pushing people aside until I'd reached her.

"Come," I said, taking her arm in mine and shoving our way back out. I could be as cold as iron when I wanted to be.

"Finally, the man's getting what he deserves," came Hector's voice loudly, near at hand. "Who did he think he was, anyway? I hope he gets put away forever."

They were heading my way, Monique smiling uneasily at Hector's declaration, her fingers gripping her glass like it might break.

I ducked away, into the nearest room, dragging Ella with me.

And there, to my surprise, at the far end, was Nicholas.

He raised one hand to me, and smiled.

In the good light I could see his face better; it was long, with a clear-angled jaw, and his smile was sweet and bright.

I glanced over my shoulder to make sure we weren't pursued. Ella needed quiet right now, not a dozen selfish condolences. I led her over to Nicholas.

"Ella, is it?" His attention turned to her tearful face.

She nodded.

"I am Nicholas Armentrout." He held out his hand.

Ella swallowed her tears and took the offered hand. "Ella Whittington."

"I'm charmed." He smiled, gently. "Now why don't you have a seat, and I'll have a drink brought in—what do you like?"

"Coffee."

"Miss Hanover?"

"The same."

"Perfect." He signaled for someone to go for the drinks. "Now what happened?"

"They arrested Leone," said Ella, her eyes fixed on the gold fabric of her dress.

Nicholas looked to me over her head.

"Fraud, I think," I replied to his silent question.

Ella sniffed and tried to wipe a tear away without our noticing.

I don't know what Nicholas's opinion was of Leone, and I imagine it wasn't a good one, but there was nothing but gentleness on his face as he moved his cane aside and leaned down to catch Ella's gaze.

"How about I tell you a story of Faerie? A true one, they say."

She looked up, hopeful. "Please."

"A true story of Faerie?" I draped my arm over my knee and leaned back in my chair. "Do tell."

"What is it?" A young lady leaned in. "What's the gossip?"

"It's not gossip, it's a story," said Nicholas. "I will tell it to you too, if you'd like."

"Stories are positively useless in a progressive society, everyone knows that," put in the lady's beau loudly, removing his cigar from his mouth to say it.

"Nonsense," said Ella. "Stories build societies."

Nicholas hid a laugh with the back of his hand.

"Go ahead," I urged.

"In days long gone, the King and Queen of Faerie had one son, their beloved prince," Nicholas began. "He was loved by his people, for he was good and gentle-hearted. When he came of age, he went to visit the outside world, as was tradition, and there he saw a beautiful young woman, a girl with soft brown hair and a voice like the singing of a brook. He loved her. He returned month after month to woo her, and the day came when he returned to Faerie with her on his arm, in a white dress, and declared that they'd been wed."

Ella's face was growing bright with interest.

"But the King of Faerie was very angry that his son chose a wife without his say, and an outworlder at that. The Faerie are proud folk and the king was used to having his way. And so, though he permitted his son to come home and to bring his wife with him, he set up a test for the girl, so that she would fail and be cast out. He held a great feast, laying out all the best food there was: meats and pastries and wine and fruit. And on the plate of his son's wife, he laid the forbidden golden pear, which none was to touch or eat save the king himself. Not knowing their customs, she ate it. And the wrath of the king was aroused and he halted the feast and demanded that she be exiled forever, as was the unmovable law."

My throat was dry. I reached for my drink and took a sip.

"The prince begged his father to reconsider. He said if there was a way that he could bring her home again, if there was a price that had to be paid, he would pay it. So the king offered his son one chance: if the prince left his home for ten years and did not return once to Faerie, but wooed his wife again, and she chose him again, then at the end of ten years, at the coming of the first snow of winter, they could return. The prince agreed."

"But when they had been cast out, he found that they had been separated. He had come to the overworld as a mere man without the powers he possessed as the prince of Faerie, and she as a rich man's daughter; and she had no memory of him. Yet he was not discouraged, but sought her out and took a job in the gardens of her father so that he could be near her. At first, she paid him no heed, but he sang as he worked, and after a time, she took notice. Now, she did not love him—at that time such a thing was not possible, a rich man's daughter and the gardener's help—but she came to love his singing. And with that he was content for many years."

"It's beautiful already," said Ella, her eyes sparkling.

"It will continue to be," said Nicholas. The coffee arrived, and we paused to pass it around.

"Sadly," Nicholas continued, when we'd properly settled, "another trial stood in their way. When seven years had passed, the prince realized that his strength was waning, being kept so long from Faerie; and the more he tried to woo her, the more he sang, the more it took from him. He became sick more and more often, and the harsh winters left him weak. Twice, the rich man's daughter tried to send him on his way in the hopes of saving his life, but he would not be parted from her."

"In the tenth year, he was so wasted with sickness that he could hardly tend the gardens. Yet he continued to sing, for his voice was untouched by his weakness. And the daughter, worried for him, found she looked forward to his song more and more each day. In the last month of his exile, four days from the time he was to have wooed her by, he collapsed in the garden. And not hearing the song, she went out to find him, afraid."

Ella was listening intently, her lips parted. As Nicholas took a drink, even I felt a flash of impatience, waiting for the end.

"She found him so weak he could not rise, fallen among the daisies, far from any help. And she realized, as she saw him dying, that she loved him. There she took his head upon her lap, and she sang to him the song he would sing to her. And as she sang his song, it freed her memory from the enchantment, and she remembered that she was his wife, and that he was the Prince of the Faeries. She knew that he must have exiled himself to come for her and that at last, it had taken everything from him. But as he lay dying, she held his hand and told him that she loved him, that he was her hero. And he whispered back that he would do it all again if it meant he could be with her a minute more. She kissed him, and then he died in her arms."

Ella gasped audibly.

"I say, I thought you said that this was a beautiful story!" protested the woman's beau, a fresh cigar grasped in his indignant fingers. Apparently, for all that "stories had no place," he was listening.

"Wait," said Nicholas. "It isn't over."

"The girl wept over the prince and sang his song as

she smoothed back his fair hair from his gentle face, and as she mourned him it came to pass that her song and her tears were heard by his mother, the queen. The queen, like many mothers, had longed for her son to return, and understood at once what had happened. Her heart was overwhelmed with grief and she came out to weep for her son and hold him in her arms. But it was she who brought about the seasons, coming to the over-world but four times a year, to bring the signs of change. And her tears became the first snow of winter, and they fell soft and gentle upon her son. And so it was that when the first snowflakes touched his cold face, he was restored to them, for he had fulfilled the terms of his exile. The queen brought her son and his love home, and when the king saw that his son had loved this girl even to death, his hardened heart was softened and he welcomed them. And ever after they lived with joy, and the prince was beloved by all."

"Oh, it was beautiful," cried Ella, tears standing in her eyes. "I'm sure it is a true story."

"They say," said Nicholas with a smile, "that the first snow is the most precious now to the faerie folk. And those who return home on that day are said to be blessed among all."

"How lovely," Ella whispered. "Thank you."

"My pleasure, of course." A gentle light shone in

Nicholas's eyes—though I suppose it always did. His suffering made him more gentle with others, not less.

They continued to talk of Faerie, and I let them be after a while. It was wearying to talk of mere fancy.

I stepped out into the fresh night, remembering for the first time in months that the night was beautiful.

"Good evening."

I almost jumped. It was Ella's pale-eyed lawyer, standing beside the decorative trees, matches and a box of cigarettes in his hand.

"Evening," I swallowed.

"Constance, right?" He tapped the box on the heel of his hand to extract a cigarette, which he placed between his lips.

"Miss Hanover, actually," I replied, with a touch of chill. I had never told him my name. In general, I never volunteered it.

"Right." He struck a match and lit the thing.

I wondered at him, so at ease among those who considered themselves his betters. He always remained professionally aloof, but I had an uneasy feeling that he, indeed, thought himself everyone else's better. There was a certain glint to his eye, a lift in the curve of his lip that gave him away.

It was disgust, I realized. Disgust with everything around him.

I felt disgusted with everything as well, myself included, but I felt no kinship in our shared feeling.

He took a long draw and breathed out a slow stream of smoke. "Hm?" He held out the cigarettes.

I put up a palm, waving them away.

He tucked them back inside the pocket of his jacket.

"Why didn't you support Ella in there?" I asked. "You are her lawyer, aren't you?"

He looked at me with a quiet, patronizing expression. "Ella is just a girl. She must learn when and when not to stand up for her friends."

"And yet you are in her employ, not her guardian."

"Her guardian is a murderer on the run. Who do you think is going to look out for her?"

He pulled the cigarette briefly from his mouth to give me a nod.

"Lovely night," he said, and moved past me, back into the roaring light of the house.

I remember thinking it was a strange thing for him to say.

Eight

*A faerie-beast creates destruction wherever it goes. It
need not try, it simply brings it in its wake. Sometimes,
all it takes to find a beast is to find the calamities.*

—A History of Faerie and the Folk

THE GOSSIP the next morning was atrocious. My
telephone rang all morning from friends, learning from
other friends that I'd seen the whole spectacle of the
arrest, wanting to know details.

After the first four or five, I told them to ask
someone else. I was tired of talking about it.

It felt too real to chatter over the telephone about in

that manner, too invasive of someone else's privacy. I went outside halfway through the morning and stayed out until evening.

That night, the party at the Chatworths was still abuzz with talk. The Wolf-Catcher was there, fending off inquiries with the protestation that his hands were full with the Sydney Whittington case and he'd had nothing to do with the arrest.

Hours later, we heard the rumble of a loud automobile approaching, and a strange feeling started inside me. I knew who it was even before the car came in view.

It was Leone.

His automobile roared up into the drive with a harsh spray of gravel. There was no woman on his arm, no one to share the attention—this was an entrance.

He shot around the fountain and ground to a halt right in front of the wide-open doors. It didn't matter a whit that he was hours late—surely he meant to be—for he threw his door wide and stepped out with more swagger than I had imagined his tall, narrow frame could carry.

Leone was wearing a smart suit (brand new), diamond cufflinks, and a wide smile. His eyes fell over the crowd just as they had when he'd first arrived with Monique on his arm: as if he was looking for trouble.

Questions pelted him as made his way up the drive and through the doors, asking if he was out on bail, who had come to his rescue, if he'd kissed anyone, if Ella had paid for him, if there were still charges, if he had to appear in court.

He just laughed at them all.

When he finally made it into the house, he went over to the host, who shook his hand a little hesitantly.

"Is Ella Whittington here?" Leone asked.

But he didn't need an answer.

"Leone!" Ella came rushing through the crowd and threw her arms around his neck.

He was laughing—he gave her a quick hug in return and stepped back.

"The charges were dropped," he announced loudly to everyone, and offering his arm to Ella, headed in the direction of the ballroom.

The lawyer followed, a silent, pale specter.

All around me, the talk burst out afresh. And his car sat in the drive, blocking the way. No one seemed to notice.

· · ·

The swift return of Leone set the entire party talking. Who had accused him? Had they dropped the charges? Was there insufficient evidence? Did Leone have shady political alliances? Was he trying to use Ella and her money for some scheme? The talk almost drowned out the music.

As for Leone, he seemed to love the attention. He told about his ordeal in great detail: the ride to the station, when he was cuffed and when he was not, the questions he'd been asked, the booking process, what his cell looked like, the evil-looking rat he chased away from his blanket.

I rather think he was exaggerating, though I cannot be sure. In any case, it made him more popular than Ella that night.

He was basking in the popularity when Hector Marion burst into the room.

"Adolphus Leone!"

"Go look over there," said Leone, jerking his head over his shoulder. "There's no Adolphus Leone here."

"You answered to that name yesterday."

"That was yesterday." Leone stretched slowly like a cat.

"Get up."

Leone didn't move, but tilted his head to fix Hector with a serious look.

"I don't have a problem with you, Mr. Marion."

"Well, I have one with you."

"Go cool off."

"Not a chance." Hector kicked the leg of Leone's chair.

Quietly, subtly, Leone gave Ella's arm a push, warning her to distance herself. She stood up and crossed the room calmly, but her eyes remained on Leone's face.

"Well, then, you had better tell me the problem. Were you the one who had me arrested yesterday?"

"Ha! I wish."

"Well, if it wasn't you, go on, then."

"I know what you do when you think no one is looking."

"How scandalous!" Leone leaned back with a grin. "Go on, this is fascinating. Expose me to everyone."

"I've seen you bribe people," he started, a little taken aback at Leone's refusal to be threatened.

"Bribe people?" Leone laughed. "Who did I bribe?"

The room laughed.

"Colonel Streatfield."

"Colonel Streatfield? Really, Marion, if you want to accuse me, accuse me of something that could be possible. He is not a man who can be bribed."

"And Monique De Flores."

"Monique?" Something flashed across Leone's face, too swift to discern. Fear, perhaps. "What has she to do with this?"

"You know very well what. You broke her heart."

"You're mad if you think I treated her ill," said Leone with a laugh. "Whatever happened between us was her choice."

"That's rot and you know it," he replied, and pulled out a derringer.

And shot him, point blank.

In hindsight, I hadn't expected a man like Hector to go through with a thing like that, even with as little respect as I had for him.

The room exploded with screams. Everyone was milling around; I saw Leone's gasping face as he slid slowly to the floor. Ella reached his side as he hit the ground, pulling aside his suit jacket, fumbling at the buttons of his shirt.

I saw something odd then: as the lawyer stepped back out of the way, his face looked concerned like the others, but his eyes—they were no longer frozen and emotionless. There was hunger in them, like an animal that's seen prey.

His eyes were on Leone.

The screams continued, and the crowd became a

crush as half the people in the room tried to flee and twice as many tried to rush in.

"Out of the way!" The Wolf-Catcher came running into the room, shoving a couple suits aside as he shed his jacket. "Give him space. Someone see if there's a doctor here!"

Ella drew back and the inspector went to his knees beside the injured man. One of Leone's fists was knotted at his side, his jaw clenched and his face white.

The Wolf-Catcher assessed the damage briefly, pulling out his handkerchief and pressing it slowly and firmly into Leone's shoulder.

Leone caught his breath in with a hiss but made no other sound.

"Can I get another handkerchief?" The Wolf-Catcher asked, loudly.

Half a dozen were presented, and a thick linen napkin. He took the napkin and added it to his own soaked handkerchief.

"How is he?" asked Ella.

"Just need to get the bleeding stopped," says the inspector, briefly. "Who shot him?"

"Hector Marion."

"Marion." He grunted as he continued to apply pressure. "Well, his marksmanship tutor probably cheated his parents."

"Is he going to be all right?" pressed Ella, trying to speak over the noise of the crowd. Someone was in hysterics.

"Someone stop that screaming!" he snapped. "He's not dying."

Relief flooded Ella's face and she did not press the inspector.

A young man with spectacles came running through the crowd, followed by an older, heavy-set man.

"Someone was shot?" the young man inquired.

"Over here," called the Wolf-Catcher. "I think it's not serious."

The doctors took over and Rothschild stood up, looking grimly into the crowd until he found Hector, flushed and angry.

"You, young man, should get on home. I will not arrest you tonight, but if Mr. Leone presses charges—"

The young man blanched. In all his spoiled life, I don't think consequences ever occurred to him. He turned and fled.

"Is it a flesh wound?" asked Leone, through his teeth.

"Yes. But the bullet is still inside you."

"How exciting," he laughed, a little breathlessly.

"We should drive you to the hospital. Does anyone have a car near at hand?"

"Take my automobile," said Ella, quickly. "My driver won't mind and the night is still young. I'll sleep here if I must."

Leone smiled, just a line in one side of his cheek. His eyes were pained, but there was warmth in his expression. "You'll have your automobile and driver back, don't you worry."

The doctors helped him up, one still pressing against the wound, and a tall young man I didn't recognize let Leone throw one arm over his shoulder and lean on him as they made their way out.

There was a hard, uncomfortable silence following their departure. Ella stood dazed, staring at a stain of blood on the carpet at her feet.

I went to her and put my hand on her shoulder. "Are you all right?"

She looked up at me, still dazed, and nodded. "He said he'd be all right."

"I am sure he will be," I replied. "You'll see."

"I don't understand it," her voice was low. "Last night he was arrested, tonight he's shot."

"It's a coincidence," I said.

"Is it?" Her eyes met mine, and there was something in them, deep and unsettled.

And then I remembered the lawyer's face.

Nine

The wonder of Faerie is written into its folk; they love sunsets and forests and flowers and mountains because they simply cannot help themselves.

—A History of Faerie and the Folk

ELLA INVITED me to her estate again later that week. I had been lounging on the terrace in the shade, doing absolutely nothing, when one of the maids came out, saying I had a visitor.

"A visitor?" I sat up and turned around at that. At least I was in a halfway decent suit.

"Yes, Miss Ella Whittington."

"No. Here?"

"Yes, ma'am. That's the name she gave. And—the face in the papers too," she added in a lower voice.

So it was Ella. I stood up and stretched. "You can bring her out here."

"Very good."

The maid left and I dragged an extra chair out next to mine and sat down. I didn't care if she saw me doing nothing. It's all I did, really.

"Constance!" Ella greeted, almost running onto the terrace. She was back to her usual bright self; the disturbed, pensive Ella I'd seen the other night was gone.

"Good morning," I replied, unfolding myself from my chair and holding out a rather limp hand.

"It is a good morning, especially since I've seen you."

That was the thing about Ella—she said rot like that, but she actually meant it.

"Anyway." She pressed her hands together. "I would like to invite you to my home to swim in the bay. Leone can't swim because he's still recovering, but he is coming, and I should love another friend along."

"I am your friend?" I couldn't help the remark—it slipped out.

"Of course!" Again, she was sincere. "Please come. Today is one of the last warm days this year."

"Hm." I inspected my nails thoughtfully. "When do you want me to come?"

"Right now, if you can. I have my automobile out front."

I hesitated, but only for a moment. "Give me ten minutes."

Her face lit up. "I'll be waiting outside."

So I went inside, up to my room, and took out my swimming costume and put on a hat.

It was truly a fine day. The water was clear and blue and gently trimmed with white, like lace on a baby's gown. The sunlight felt like golden nectar, soaking the hot sand, the beach chairs, the umbrellas in its burning light.

"The sea is quiet today," Ella said as we crossed the sand, shading her eyes and looking out at the lapping water. "It will be ideal for swimming. Did you swim much, growing up?"

"All the time. Our house stands on the bay."

"I wasn't permitted to swim much," Ella replied. "Though I didn't mind terribly—I loved the forest more, and father allowed that."

Her face lit bright as the sun when she said that.

A sharp bark greeted us from the terrace and a young sheepdog came bounding down to greet us.

"You didn't tell me you had a dog," I replied, taking a sharp step sideways to avoid it.

"I didn't have him last week," Ella laughed, reaching down to scratch its ears with one hand. "He is from an admirer."

"Do you know who?" I glanced over at her, again sidestepping the dog.

"Anonymous!" She laughed and knelt down to rub its head with both hands.

"Does he have a name?"

"Prince." She shook her long golden hair out of her face. "Isn't he lovely?"

He was, in his way. As long as he stayed where he was, by Ella, and didn't get too close. I wasn't used to dogs—my mother did not allow them—though once, a very long time ago, I had asked for a puppy.

Marge and I had both begged and been denied.

"Run off now, Prince!" Ella stood up smiling, a little breathless. The dog happily went its way, sniffing through all the shrubbery, and we turned to continue our trek across the sand.

"Oh dear," whispered Ella, as our eyes fell upon the arrangement before us on the beach.

Leone lay in a long chair, his legs crossed and hanging off the end. His shirt was half undone, and under the windblown edge I saw a thick bandage across his shoulder and chest.

"You told me you were coming later," said Ella reproachfully, stopping next to him.

He shrugged and squinted up at her, remorseless. "I was bored. What else was I going to do?"

She laughed, then shook her head, scolding but not annoyed. "It is respectful to give notice, is all. Don't you have any other sort of life?"

"Not at present."

"I suppose you want me to feel sorry for you?"

Leone grinned slowly.

"Well, I don't." Ella turned her back on him. "You'll have to wait—Constance and I are going swimming!"

I had not been swimming at all that season, and I'd forgotten how good it felt to dive into cool, clear water, feel the tang of salt on your lips as you surface, surrounded by frothing, swelling waves. And all with the bright, hot sun beating chummily on your shoulders.

I used to love that feeling.

"Are you tired yet?" Ella sat on the edge of the swimming platform, anchored some thirty meters offshore. Her damp hair caught the breeze like spinning gold.

"I could go much longer," I admitted, reaching up to take hold of the side of the platform. "But if you are tired, by all means—"

"I am not tired." Ella shook her head and drew her knees up to her chin.

I gripped the edge of the platform and pulled myself up beside her. The planks were hot from the sun and I stretched myself out, leaning my chin on my arms.

"Do you ever feel things and you don't know why?" Ella asked. "Or catch the corner of a memory, and you cannot place it?"

"Sometimes."

"Hm." She laughed softly through her nose. "Are they—good or bad?"

"Both, I think. Why do you ask?"

But she just shrugged. "Leone looks rather alone, there on the beach by himself," she commented with a little smile. "Poor fellow."

"Is he healing all right?"

"I don't know."

"Have you not seen him much?"

"No, plenty. He says he is all right, but when he thinks I'm not looking—I think it hurts him badly."

"It's only been a few days."

Ella nodded, but there was still worry behind her eyes.

On the shore, servants emerged from the house, carrying what promised to be a picnic.

"Come," she said, getting to her feet. "Let's swim back and have lunch and then we can swim some more. We can't leave all the food for Leone!"

Ella dove into the water, disappearing under its clear, glittering surface.

"Wonders never cease," teased Leone as we emerged from the sea and ran for our towels. "Here I was, lonely, and the sea spits out two beautiful young ladies."

I shot him a look, but it didn't seem to bother him. Ella giggled.

He had found the dog—or rather, the dog had found him, for he hadn't stirred from his chair. It was sitting beside him, tail wagging, its eyes fastened upon a tennis ball in his hand.

"Go on, Rover!" He tossed it down towards the water and the dog scrambled after it.

"His name is Prince," said Ella. "Didn't I tell you that?"

"Might have. I've a terrible memory."

"Excuses," she declared, unconcerned, pulling over a beach chair to be closer to him. "Perhaps you would have a better memory if you applied yourself to things other than lounging and going to parties."

"You go to them," protested Leone. "The parties."

"If I didn't, I wouldn't see you. Or her. Or any of the others, like Colonel Streatfield."

"Not missing much," he muttered.

"Why do you even put up with us, Ella?" I was tilting my head sideways, trying to get the water out of my ears.

Ella smiled and shook her head, as if no answer was needed.

"Yes, why do you put up with us?" urged Leone, a grin to match the panting dog's on his face. "Come on, Ella!"

"Miss Whittington," she corrected. "Mind your place."

"My place? I thought we'd agreed I could call you Ella."

"Only when you behave, and you've come two hours early."

"I see." He pitched the ball petulantly. "Is that food ready?"

I craned my neck to see into the garden; the servants were still in the middle of preparations. Leone took my expression, whatever it was, as a no.

The dog came back up to us, dripping saltwater, and deposited the ball beside Leone.

"Surely you have other reasons for being with us, Miss Whittington. We're such bores...Miss Hanover excluded." He pitched the ball after the dog.

Ella did not take the bait. But she did laugh, and as she did, something like fear shot through her eyes.

At the time, I was sure I had imagined it.

Luncheon was served in the corner of the garden closest to the beach: sandwiches, lemonade, and pound cake.

"This is my favorite," Ella declared, looking around with an air of contentment. "Just me, a couple friends, and the wind in the trees."

Leone craned his neck around to look at the trees, moving a little gingerly. His brow suddenly furrowed. "He's at it again," he said. "That old scarecrow is watching us."

I followed his gaze up to one of the second-floor windows. The lawyer stood there, framed by the curtains, his frosty gaze lingering on our small party.

"Ignore him," said Ella. "He's just nosy and protective."

"He should learn better. Nosy gets you into places

you don't want to be." Leone rubbed the back of his neck ruefully.

It seemed to me the look of a man who knew from personal experience.

"Don't underestimate him," said Ella seriously, reaching to refill her glass of lemonade. "I don't think he likes to be crossed."

"Aw, I could take him any day."

Ella sipped her lemonade in silence and looked out towards the bay.

"Tea, miss," announced one of the servants, coming out with a full tray.

"Thank you." Ella glanced up, pushing her hair back, and gave the woman the kindest smile. I don't know how she managed being so everlastingly kind.

Leone pushed the cake over to make room for the tray, but the servant simply set the cups in front of us, already full.

"Do you need anything else, miss?" she asked.

"No, this is lovely."

"Miss." The woman gave a bob and took the empty tray back up to the house.

"Very kind of them, pouring out for us," said Leone. His eyes went slowly around the garden as he stirred his tea.

"They don't usually," said Ella, perplexed, as she took a sip. "I didn't ask them to."

"Hm." Leone tapped his spoon on the edge of his teacup and set it down on his plate.

If the dog had not suddenly looked up, I would have missed it: Leone, swift and practiced and almost too smooth, poured his tea into the gardenias.

A cold jolt went through me, and I looked at my own tea.

But Ella was still drinking hers, and I had taken several sips already and felt fine.

He picked up a sandwich and continued as though nothing had happened, but what I had seen didn't sit well with me.

After eating, we went back to sit on the beach and sip our lemonades.

"Aren't you tired, Leone?" asked Ella, watching as he laid back against the chair, biting back a grimace.

So it did pain him.

"Nonsense, I am more than well." His face cleared immediately, like a curtain being drawn back.

"I don't think you are."

"Well, I cannot stay for dinner, so I am determined to make your life exciting while I can."

"I wish you would stay for dinner sometime. You've never been in the house."

"Someday I will. I just get so frightfully bored of indoor spaces when there isn't a party." Leone scratched his neck sheepishly.

Ella turned to me, suddenly eager. "Constance, could you stay?"

"I—suppose so." I shrugged.

"Will your mother be worried if you stay late?" Her hand paused on her glass.

"No. She hasn't a clue half the time where I am or what I am doing."

She took a sip. "I wish I had that kind of freedom."

"And what would you do if you had that kind of freedom?" asked Leone.

"I'd run in open fields and pick flowers and lie in the grass until the day faded and the stars came out over the top of me."

"A regular faerie-child."

"You shouldn't joke like that," said Ella, with a quick glance over at me. "Especially with all the rumors that fly about...regarding Sydney."

"He brought them on himself, the stuffed shirt."

"Leone!"

"You should be kind to me, Miss Whittington. I've been hurt, you know." His manner switched to mock innocence faster than the switch of an electric bulb.

"I have been very kind to you, Leone. You know that. But you should know better by now than to insult my family."

"I beg your pardon. But you must know, he irks me sorely." He raised his glass to his lips and took a generous swallow.

"You two should have a swimming race," Leone proposed, setting aside his lemonade with sudden conviction. "Out to the platform and back."

"You can't be serious!" protested Ella.

"We would have to set another marker," I said. "It's far too shallow by the shore. We'd be ending in a footrace."

"Easy. I will go stand as the marker. Up to my waist should do."

"You cannot get your bandages wet," warned Ella.

"I was shot in the shoulder, not the stomach. Let's live a little."

Ella glanced at me.

"Sure." I tucked my long arms behind my head and leaned back. "But make it from the platform to shore—I'm far too tired to race both ways."

·   ·   ·

We dove from the platform in the last golden light of the day, cutting clean as knives under the sea.

When I came up, I could see Leone standing in the rising waves, holding the ball. The sheepdog was splashing in the shallows.

I am not, in general, a competitive person—there are far more important things in life to bother about. But our judge had a clear favorite, and I found myself inclined to prove him wrong, so I settled into a strong, pulling stroke with a mind to win.

Leone was shouting, his words indistinguishable from under the waves, and a glance behind me showed me that I had a slim lead.

I pressed on faster, and his shouting increased—he must have been cheering on Ella. The waves were tinged with gold, the air had the faintest chill above the warmth of the shallowing water, and I had a good sort of ache in my arms, as if I'd earned being tired. It felt wonderful.

I crossed the line, a length and a half ahead, and sprang up, sloughing the water from my face.

Ella crossed a moment later with a steady, calm stroke.

"No, no, back the other way!" Leone shouted, tossing the ball hand to hand.

I put my hands on my hips and shot him a look.

"No, I'm done!" Ella stood up with a gasp.

"I'd have liked to see you go a little farther," he said. "Perhaps you would have caught her."

"It's easy for you to say, standing there doing nothing," Ella scolded, laughing as she wrung out her hair.

"It's always easy for me to say," he replied, a half-grin starting in one corner of his mouth. "It just comes out, easy as breathing."

"Oh, hush."

We all started for the shore, wading against the swelling waves. Soon the tide would be coming in.

On the beach, as we gathered our things, I glanced back—why, I do not know—and was struck by the rich, sherbet light of the setting sun.

It was only for a moment—but I suddenly remembered Marge. We'd played by the sea often as little girls, but there was one summer night when we'd played until the sun touched the horizon.

I remembered how free I'd felt. Like I could have spread my arms and flown straight into the pink and gold clouds.

I told her I'd never felt this happy.

And Marge had laughed and said she'd never been that happy either. Just because we had each other and we'd had a marvelous day.

A sick feeling rose in my chest. As if I'd remembered something bad, something that had gone horribly wrong.

"Constance!" Ella had turned around, shading her eyes against the setting sun to look at me. I stuck my hands in the pockets of my outer wrap and trudged on.

The moment passed.

Ten

*The folk of Faerie do not like to deal in secrets.
However, when needed, a secret may be buried as safely
inside them as if it were buried in the heart of the earth.*

—A History of Faerie and the Folk

I WAS SURPRISED to see Inspector Rothschild at the
next party I attended. It was small, and his presence was
sure to be noticed and commented upon in such a small
company; and yet there he was.

I ran into him in the hall between the dining room
and the ballroom, his signature untouched glass in his
hand.

"Inspector!" I held out my hand with a smile. "I haven't seen you recently. I thought perhaps you had found success elsewhere?"

He gave me a long, wry look, then gave a laugh through his nose and shook his head. "Wouldn't that be the day. Sydney Whittington knows how to disappear into thin air. He's done it before, just—not with a murder charge on his head."

"I see."

"Strange man. You ever see his acts?"

"Yes, quite a few times."

"People say his father didn't approve of his stage career. Thought it demeaned the family."

"Do you think that?"

"That's a question for you to answer. I have never been—" He cleared his throat and glanced around at the decor. "This."

"I think it is the luxury of the rich to do as they please. But my mother finds me irresponsible and progressive."

He raised his eyebrows, whether in approval or disapproval I could not tell.

"Do the police really think that this is a good use of your time, to shadow Ella?"

"There's proof that they've been corresponding. Not everything is as it seems on the surface, I can tell you that." He took a sip, a real sip, of his drink. "I see you have been spending time with her."

"She needs a friend. One that doesn't need or want her money."

He just nods.

"If things are not as they seem, may I surmise that Ella is not the only one you're watching?"

"I see you are doing some watching of your own."

"I see you have avoided my question, no offense meant."

He laughed, genuinely this time. "Miss Hanover, I think you're sharper than you let on."

"Flattered, then. I must reciprocate." Reciprocate, but also escape the scrutiny. I hold up my glass. "They say that you have no fear."

He smiled wearily, as if it was a compliment, but a false one. "It was true, once."

"And not now?" I raised my eyebrows and bit back a smile. "Do tell."

"It's neither scandalous nor interesting." I heard a touch of reproof in his voice. "I am getting too old for this job, that's all."

"Age does not make one afraid," I pushed back. "Look at Colonel Streatfield over yonder."

Rothschild spared him a glance.

"No, age does not make you afraid, but sometimes it

makes you appreciate what there is to fear. I was married later in life, Miss Hanover. I have a young daughter. And every night when I go out, and she throws her arms around my neck and gives me a kiss, I tell her I will see her in the morning when she wakes. And every night, I fear I have lied to her."

He took a hard, short sip of his drink and hissed through his teeth. "That's where fear comes into it."

"You've come home so far, and you've had a long career."

"It doesn't matter. I see it every day—people who never come home. Death isn't particular."

"I see."

I suppose that went for Marge too. I certainly never thought she'd go that way or so soon. I suppose most of us don't think of it until we're forced to.

"I should let you enjoy your evening." He gave me an apologetic smile. I wonder if my musings showed on my face.

"Thank you." I extended my glass to his. "I'll enjoy it about as much as you will, I expect."

I continued down the hall and into a large sitting room where Ella and Leone held court. Even with a smaller party, there were nearly a dozen people to be found around them, engaged in a roaring discussion.

"I still say," one young man was saying, "that the

artists are the ones you have to be careful of. The magic may have addled his brain. Magicians are known to be unstable."

"He was a magnificent showman," said a girl across the room. "Hardly the unstable sort. I've seen addled artists—my cousin was one."

I stepped into the room and the lawyer moved aside to let me through. He gave me a brief nod.

"The best ones always are," said Leone in a teasing voice.

"You too?" She turned on him, but her eyes were sparkling.

"Your brother was a fraud," he continued, with a little, white smile. "Didn't you know he lied about his age in order to get his stage license early?"

"I didn't." A small frown started between her brows, though her lips were smiling. "Are you sure about that, Leone?"

"It was practically common knowledge." Leone took a sheepish sip of his drink, trying to hide, I think, his pleasure in further toppling Sydney.

"I don't believe it," said Ella, shaking her head. "I don't know where you get all your gossip from."

"True sources," he said. "True sources."

"I believe it when you prove it."

"Ella makes a fair point, Mr. Leone," I said, seating

myself gracefully on the edge of an empty chair, "You seem to have an awful lot of talk in you and I have yet to see facts to back it up."

"I'm wild, Miss Hanover, I can't help it." He leaned back on the sofa, one arm dangling lazily over the arm. His other arm was around Ella's shoulder.

"That is no excuse." I draped my arms over my knees. "You can fleece everyone else, but me—you have to prove it."

He gave me the strangest look then, as if trying to tell if I was serious. Or perhaps if I meant more by the remark.

"I've had enough of this," said Leone, standing up and reaching out his hand for Ella. "Who wants to dance?"

Ella lit up at this remark and led the way out of the door.

I was not in the mood to dance, so I was one of the last to stand.

Leone had left Ella's side and gone over to the mantel—I registered the action as odd a bare moment before he reached behind the decorative clock. I only saw it as a flash of white. A piece of paper.

His hand closed slowly and went to his pocket. When it reappeared a minute later, casually, it was empty.

No one else seemed to notice as they were emptying the room. I lingered beside the door as Leone went over to the table to retrieve his glass.

He'd actually sipped it that night, it was only half full.

Turning, he realized I was lingering.

"What are you looking at, Miss Hanover?" He took a step towards me and there was a different glint in his eye, a kind of knife-like intensity.

"You, sir." I drew myself up coldly.

"Well, you'd better think carefully about that."

"What, is that a threat?"

"No." He smiled, faintly. "It's a warning."

He didn't give me a chance to answer. He strode from the room with his head lifted, refusing to acknowledge me further.

Eleven

There are places in the world where the veil between Earth and Faerie is very thin. And a person may glimpse, if careful, the gleam of far-off wonders.

—A History of Faerie and the Folk

WHEN AN INVITATION CAME from Ella three days later to come on a picnic with her and Leone, I accepted it immediately. I could not always keep an eye on her, but after that night at the party, I much preferred the idea of being with her when Leone was there.

They picked me up in Leone's automobile, a fast, sleek model with no roof. I don't know how he could afford it, if rumors about the state of his finances were true.

This did not seem to bother Ella, though perhaps as a girl of sixteen she didn't think about it.

"Climb in!" cried Ella with a laugh. "You'll have to excuse the basket."

I moved the picnic basket to the other side of the seat and settled myself beside it.

"Hang on, girls," said Leone with a grin, and he tore out of our drive.

I do rather hope mother was out. That is always how Marge left. And I do think those reminders gave her grief.

"Where are we going?" I called over the rush of the wind. Leone was going fast.

"I thought we'd drive out of the city and find some open meadow," he shouted back, a little smile on his face.

"Out of the city!" cried Ella with rapture.

The meadow we found was strewn with daisies and other wildflowers, caught between the road and a forest.

Ella declared it perfect.

We laid a blanket in the grass and set out the food as

Ella picked an armful of daisies. There were sand-wiches, pickles, fruit, and cake.

"Isn't it delightful?" asked Ella. "Leone brought it all."

"You?" I turned to him with raised eyebrows. "Where from?"

"I made it." He sounded offended. "Or, you know—bought some of it."

"Hm."

Ella reached for a sandwich and took a small bite. "It's delightful, Leone. I love it."

I reached for a cherry, unimpressed.

After we ate, Leone stood up and brushed the crumbs off of his legs.

"Ladies, I am going to take a stroll and fetch the key from the auto. I forgot it."

"Be careful—of the road," said Ella. "Some people drive fearfully fast."

"I haven't met the man yet who can take me down." He winked as he turned away.

"Why do you like him?" I asked, watching his retreating back. He was tall and good-looking, charming, but these were things that didn't seem important to Ella.

At least, she didn't seem smitten in that way.

"He is kind to me." She picked an apple out of the

picnic basket. "And he is ever so much fun to be around."

"Does he ever talk about—the future?"

"No, he doesn't," she insisted, laughing with the faintest touch of exasperation. "I try to tell people that."

"All the worse for you if he doesn't," I replied. "You are too good for a man who has no intentions of commitment."

She took this from me quietly, twisting her golden hair around her fingertip.

"But he's gentle," she countered softly. "And I think he is committed to me, in his way. Sometimes he gets a look in his eye like he'd die for me if I gave him the chance."

"He'd die for your money, you mean."

"No." Her voice was very quiet, but firm. "For me."

She took a pensive bite of her apple. "And he makes me laugh."

"As does every other social climbing young rake."

"There are worse things," she said. "I want to laugh again. It may not look like it, but I am so very sad about my father still. Leone helps me feel better."

"I'm just not sure he is a good person to spend so much of your time with."

"Hm." She took a bite of the apple and leaned back

onto the grass, her golden hair spread out around her like a crown.

"He doesn't strike me as the sort who is entirely safe. You can't deny there's a wildness about him."

"True, but if I am already in danger, being around someone who can take care of themselves like that is the best thing, don't you think?"

"What makes you think you are in danger?"

"My father."

"Because they suspect he was murdered?"

"That's the thing...it was murder. I am sure of that."

"Does that bother you?"

"All the time." She pulled up a couple blades of grass and wound them around her finger. "I am sure now that it wasn't Sydney, and the police have no other suspect. It's very careless of them."

"That or whoever did it was extremely clever."

A shadow fell over her face.

"What is it?"

"Nothing."

"Could it have been done by a member of the staff? Your lawyer, perhaps." His pale eyes swam into my mind's eye.

"No. He was on business in Clearside. It's an hour's drive, he couldn't have been there."

"Did your father have guests?"

"Just Sydney, I think."

"Did your father ever have enemies?"

"No. He was strict and didn't go anywhere."

"That could have meant he had enemies once. Men who keep to themselves often have secrets."

"I think he was just protective. He could be like that. Never wanting me to go anywhere, always saying that if I went out I'd become like Sydney and leave him. He always said he wanted me to stay."

"Interesting." I reached into the basket and pulled out the bowl of cherries. "And did you mind that?"

"Not really—no, yes, I did. But I am still young. I just supposed father and I would have it out once I was grown. I'm rather sorry now that we never will, though I did so dread it."

She took one last bite of the apple and threw it into the grass. "Just think, in a few years that could be an apple tree."

"I'm going to take a walk." I stood up, brushing my skirt off.

"Enjoy it. I am going to take a nap among the daisies."

"Where has Leone got to?" I shaded my eyes, looking for his tall, golden-haired figure first by the automobile, then the road.

"I thought he was getting something out of the automobile."

"It seems like it's been too long for that."

"Maybe." Ella lay back on the grass and threw her arm over her eyes. "Enjoy your walk."

"Thank you."

With a whisper of unquiet beginning in my mind, I headed off across the meadow towards the woods.

I had never been a great one for the outdoors, as some girls are, but we had never been on bad terms either, and I liked a good stroll. And the woods looked pleasant and ruddy, full of the colors of the season. Exactly the kind of thing you wanted over your head, mingling with the blinding blue sky. The woods themselves were still in leaf, though the leaves were turning, and through them, just a glimpse could be seen of a shining lake.

How delicious.

The shore seemed close enough—five minutes of walking should do the trick, I thought. I started through the trees. Birds were singing, and small animals, rabbits or squirrels or the like, rustled loudly in the underbrush, probably foraging before winter came.

It was peaceful. I could not remember a time—recently, at least—that I had felt so calm.

The lake shimmered through the trees ahead of me, silver and tantalizing.

And then I realized it had been more than five minutes, and still the shore looked no nearer.

I glanced behind me. I could barely see the glimmer of light through the trees where I'd entered.

An odd chill went through me, and I suddenly felt very sure that it would make no difference how far I walked. I had heard stories of such strange things, but had always thought them foolish.

"Constance!" It was Ella calling, far behind me.

"Coming!" I called back.

With one glance back at the shimmering lake, I turned to walk back.

Whatever it was I had seen, it would remain in my mind as a question—no, more of a wonder—the day I glimpsed something far-off and beautiful.

"We're leaving," said Leone when I got back to the picnicking spot. He was folding up the blanket.

"I thought you said we were going to stay all afternoon."

"Well, I—" There was something suppressed in his manner.

"I wanted to go," Ella supplied quickly. "I didn't want to be out too late."

"Ah. Is—something the matter?"

"I don't think so," said Leone lightly. "Are you worried it will rain?" He squinted up at the nearly cloudless sky. "Come, Ella."

I trailed them to the automobile. Whatever they said, there was something a little changed in their manner, and I didn't like it.

We packed up the car, the two of them laughing and talking and I squeezing myself in next to the basket again, and we left.

"Did you ever picnic out here before, Miss Hanover?" asked Leone as we sped down the road.

"Now and then," I said.

The last time had been with Marge and a few of our mutual friends. By the time the picnic was finished, they were no longer my friends; and it was one of the last times Marge and I had spent together.

"But picnicking made people cross and uncomfortable," I said. "It usually caused more unpleasantness than it was worth."

Leone laughed and pressed the accelerator.

The landscape blurred past us.

He turned to Ella and shouted something that I couldn't quite make out.

She laughed. "Leone, stop, you're going too fast!"

He grinned in response, but the car did not slow down.

"Leone!"

His smile froze on his face. His eyes flicked down to his feet. I realized then that he'd already been pressing the brakes.

Nothing was happening.

He laughed, catching his composure up again, and there was a bold sort of bravery in his expression. It was the first time I saw how a girl might fall hard for him.

"Hang on, Ella, I'm not going to let anything happen to you."

Her face was white, her fingers gripping the side of the door fiercely.

We careened down the road, Leone running us into the grass on the side, trying to slow us. We were coming to a fork in the road with a fenced field directly in front of us, and I doubted we could make the turn in either direction with overturning the car.

"Hold tight," Leone shouted.

We smashed through the field gate, the windshield shattering around us. I threw up my arms and ducked. The world jolted, rose, and then came to a rakish halt.

We'd torn through mud and partway up a hill. That and the gate had helped to slow us.

The car was steaming out the front; mud and glass were spread all around us. The contents of the basket now shared the floor with my feet, mixed with shards of glass.

Ella threw open her door and fled the automobile, her breath shaking.

Leone was white as chalk and trying to catch his breath. For a moment, he could only sit there, and I thought perhaps he was about to faint. He hardly looked like himself.

But then he took a long, deep breath, and the color returned to his face and the pain written across it disappeared.

He got out of the car and ran to Ella, who was crouched on the ground panting, her hands closed into fists.

"Are you hurt?" He examined her closely, reaching up to move her hair back out of her face, looking for cuts or bruises.

Ella held out her hands, opening them, looking at her bloody palms as they shook.

"Oh, Ella." He reached swiftly for her hands, cupping them in his. "Is that all?"

"I think so," she whispered.

"Let me check."

Gently he reached under her elbows and helped her

to her feet, examining her closely and having her move each limb.

"The hands are enough," he said, when he was satisfied that she was not hurt any worse. "And I'll have those taken care of."

He turned to look at me, over his shoulder. "Miss Hanover?"

"I am all right." My limbs all worked, but I already knew my back was going to be dreadfully sore.

He turned, giving me the honor of his full, earnest gaze. "Are you sure?"

"Yes." I reached up and rubbed my neck. My heart was still hammering and my hands were shaking dreadfully.

Leone pulled his handkerchief out of his pocket, shaking it out and laying it gently over one of Ella's hands.

"It's all right, it's over." He put his arm around her shoulders and drew her close.

"Hey! Are you folks all right?"

A car was idling on the road where we'd smashed the gate. A tall man was the driver, and beside him rode a woman in a wide hat.

"None badly injured," called back Leone. "Had a problem with the brakes."

He turned quietly to Ella. "Come."

He walked Ella down to the idling car, and the driver followed him back up the hill to look over the wreck.

"There's room for you, miss," our benefactor said, touching the brim of his hat. "Are you hurt?"

"No," I answered. A smattering of little cuts on my arms stung like fire, but none of them were bleeding enough to be of concern.

I was still too dazed to think clearly.

"Well, we'll salvage your things and then take you back home. Head down to the car and catch your breath for a bit—there's no need for you to wait for us."

So I wandered back across the field towards the road. My dress was torn and smelled of gasoline and fresh dirt.

"Poor darling," said the woman, when I reached the car. "Are you hurt?"

I shook my head. I didn't know what I was.

They drove us back to Ella's house, where she loaned us her automobile to go home.

"Do you need any help with your hands?" I asked.

"No, just go home," she said quietly. She'd been subdued, shaken since the wreck. "Leone can drive you."

I was not particularly eager to drive home with Leone, but I certainly wasn't going to call home for our car. The less my parents knew about this, the better.

The moment I'd shut the car door and it was just the two of us, I turned to Leone. "What was all that?"

"What do you mean?"

"The brakes?"

He looked at me strangely and then my meaning dawned on him.

"You really think I would cut my own brakes?"

"You tell me. As I recall, you were the only one alone with the automobile during the picnic."

"That doesn't mean anything."

"How do you explain it?"

"There were times when none of us were around the vehicle."

"Who could it possibly have been? We were out in the middle of nowhere."

"Look, I—" He glanced over at me and went silent, seeming to reconsider whatever excuse he had planned to make.

"You may be able to fool Ella because she is young and sheltered, but you cannot fool me."

"Is that what you think, Miss Hanover? That I am trying to fool Ella?"

"Look me in the face and tell me it's a lie, then."

He kept his eyes on the road.

"Look me in the eye," I repeated.

He pulled into my drive and put on the brake.

"Your stop, Miss Hanover." His face was blank and hard.

I got out and slammed the door.

Inside, I went straight for the stairs.

"Constance is that you?"

"Yes, mother."

I took my muddy shoes off right away and quickened my stride, wincing at pain in my ankle. As the excitement was wearing off, new things began to hurt.

"How was your day?" Her voice trailed me up the stairs.

"Fine," I replied. The last thing mother needed to know was that I'd been in an automobile accident.

"I want a hot bath drawn," I told the first cleaning girl I ran across.

"Are you all right, miss?" she asked.

"Yes, it's nothing, just a little trouble on the road. Don't tell mother—she bought me this dress."

"Yes, miss."

"And hurry with the bath," I called after her.

I stayed in my room until the bath had been drawn,

in case Mother happened to be about. Then I grabbed a change of clothes and ran down the hall in my bare feet, wincing all the way.

I was going to be very sore for the rest of the week.

I shut the door and threw the fresh dress over the chair. The water steamed, hot and inviting, and I just sat staring at it for the longest time, trailing my fingers in it.

All this time I'd wanted to feel something. But not even a brush with death had brought it back. All I felt now was how much my chest moved with every breath, and how real and close the water looked. The cool porcelain against my wrist and the scald of the hot water on my fingers.

That was real. I still didn't feel anything, but it was very real.

After a time, someone knocked on the door.

"Busy," I murmured, just loud enough to be heard, my eyes still staring vacantly at the water. They left me alone, whoever they were.

But the disturbance was just enough to rouse me. I stood up, shed the dress ruined with grass and dirt and motor oil and ground-up glass, and slipped into the warm water.

It enveloped me and I let it.

Twelve

It has been said that at times and places in history, that faeries have fallen in love with mortals, and wed them. But there is always a price to be paid.

—A History of Faerie and the Folk

"Constance, another invitation has come for you!"

My mother's voice rang up the stairs.

I sat up and groaned. I was sore from head to toe. Despite the long, hot bath with salts, everything had screamed when I woke up today, so I hadn't even tried to get up.

"Should I throw it out? It's from Senator Armentrout. The man had no interest in parties until the election year came up. Really, I—"

I sprang up, throwing on a wrap.

"Mother, may I see it?" I called, hurrying out to the head of the stairs.

"Of course, I'll leave it just here. I am heading out for the day."

"Thank you."

I hesitated. I wasn't sure how going up and down stairs was going to agree with me yet, and I didn't want an audience. Perhaps if I waited a minute she'd just sail out.

"You know, Constance." My mother paused at the door. "I am surprised you have any interest in going to the Armentrouts'. It's likely to be all for politics."

"It is," I agreed. "But I am friends with his son now."

"Oh?" She raised one eyebrow, slow and dignified, as only a mother can.

"No, nothing like that. He's unspoiled and not wild and—I'm tired of wild people." It just slipped out.

But I was. And I felt it in that moment with such conviction.

"Good." It was the only thing her shocked lips could form. "Well, if that's the case, have him to dinner sometime, won't you? I want to meet a young man who isn't wild. Perhaps I'll even vote for his father."

She gave me a hopeful little smile and left.

I waited until I could hear the automobile leaving and then I eased my way down the stairs. I felt rather like an awkward stork, arms and legs sticking out stiffly.

I tore open the cream envelope and pulled it out.

Friday, the twelfth.

I would surely go.

Upstairs, I decided to work on yesterday's damage while mother was out. I bundled up the dress, deciding it was too ripped to save, and gave it to one of our most trusted maids with instructions to dispose of it far away from mother's eye.

She didn't need an explanation to understand.

I checked every tiny pinprick of a cut and washed them all. They'd heal up fast, but for the next week or two, there'd be no sleeveless dresses.

"Miss Constance." A small rap sounded on the door.

I limped over and opened it.

One of the maids was standing there, holding my purse.

"Excuse me, but a gentleman dropped by. Said he met you yesterday and helped you in a spot, and you'd left your handbag behind in his automobile."

"Oh." I had. I'd been so dazed I hadn't even remembered it. "Thank you."

"Yes'm."

I limped back to the bed and threw the handbag down. Call me cynical, but I thought it would be wise to check and make sure everything was still there.

I reached in and my fingers hit paper.

It was a diary. Small, brown, well-made. It had a cluster of daisies painted on the front—hand-painted, it looked like.

I flipped it open, looking for a name or something to identify it.

The handwriting inside was bold and slanted. A man's hand.

Dearest little one, the entry read, *please forgive my delay in writing to you. I was waylaid, and it will make for an exciting story, but not today. I must be brief.*

I flipped the page.

The next entry was a different hand, larger and more childish.

Dear Brother, I wish you would let me meet you properly. I know what you will say—that until I am sixteen, father's wishes are the most important of all. But I hardly remember you.

Below that, in the former hand came a reply.

You do not need more than you have. Contentment,

dear sister, will teach you far more than anything I could impart in person. I know that waiting will not be easy, but it will be worth it.

I turned more pages, skimming, looking for something that would indicate the owner. I was, of course, beginning to have my suspicions.

You will not remember it, you were so little, but one time you found a burst of daisies in the yard and you played so long in them that you fell asleep. And I carried you in.

In small, girlish handwriting below this entry: *I remember.*

More pages.

You say that your governess lets you read A History of Faerie and the Folk—what story do you love best? You must guess mine.

If you ever doubt, remember that I would fight an army for you, little sister.

—Sydney

So it was Sydney and Ella. Some private correspondence that spanned years, it seemed. Near the end of the book, I found an entry on its own, scrawled hastily.

Please wait for me and do not leave on your own. If you leave, he can catch you.

Your loving brother, S.

I flipped quickly to the next page, but it was empty.

And the one after that. I turned every page, but there was nothing. The diary had stopped.

But in the very end of the book, tucked between the last pages, was a small note written on a piece of torn stationary.

Think again before you cross me. I can do worse than the brakes. You think that I don't see your every move?

I slammed the book shut. I had to warn Ella.

She came the next day, for tea. I was glad Mother was out—Ella still had bandages on her hands, and Mother was the type of person to inquire about it.

I waited only until the pleasantries were over to show her the diary, lest she think there was anything untoward in my reasons for inviting her.

"This was brought by the man who gave us a lift home after the automobile accident," I said, handing her the diary. "I assume it is yours?"

"Yes." She fingered the cover. "Did you read it?"

"Only enough to know what it is."

"You cannot tell anyone that we had contact after my father's murder. You must not. Sydney could be in terrible danger, worse than me."

"I think they already know. Inspector Rothschild told me you were in contact."

"Oh no. If he knows, who else does?"

"I would imagine as he's the inspector, he knows more than most."

"Even so...." Ella bit her knuckle.

Then a sparkle crept into her eyes. "It was a very good little method, wasn't it? Writing to each other in a book."

"Very clever," I conceded. "How long have you kept this correspondence up?"

"It started a couple years after my mother died. I was only five when she passed, and my father strictly forbade anyone from talking about her. I think it was around then that he kept me from seeing Sydney."

"Were there suspicious circumstances around your mother's death?"

"No, not that I know of. She was not in good health during my lifetime—often stayed in bed, and I wasn't allowed to see her often because she tired easily. But by all accounts, Father adored her. And when she died, he simply wasn't the same person anymore. He could not stand to hear her name because losing her was so hard, and so with her, part of him died too."

"So you don't know much about her?"

"No. But Sydney promised to tell me more about her when I'd grown and could do what I wished. I think, for all that they disagreed, he understood Father in a way that no one else did."

"Are they much alike?"

"My brother is a perfect mix of both my parents, so I understand. My father was much gentler before my mother's death. But serious, like Sydney."

I showed her Sydney's last entry and then the note.

The last entry she shrugged at, and the note she fingered slowly. She did not seem as worried as I thought she would be.

"Someone did sabotage the automobile," I said.

"Yes...."

"You guessed that?"

"Well, I wondered."

"Do you know who it is? Or to whom your brother was referring in his note to you?"

"He wrote that note a long time ago, just days after Father died," she said. "I've been waiting since. Sydney can't just show up, you know."

"But aren't you worried someone is after you? This can't wait. What if it was the person who killed your father? After your inheritance, perhaps?"

"Perhaps." She seemed unwilling to commit.

"Ella, you must take this seriously."

"Sometimes you have to make your own decisions to protect the ones you love," she said stolidly.

"Yes, but don't you think that perhaps, in this case, it is better to let your brother handle it? You are sixteen and you live surrounded by—" I bit back the word *fools*. "By people who don't actually care."

"You care. That counts for something."

"Yes, but I am one person." I fold my arms. "And I can only do so much when you live practically on your own."

"I am safer in public," she said. "There I can see everyone and everyone can see me."

"And also get to you easier. You can't ignore this threat, Ella."

"I'm not ignoring it," replied Ella, twisting her golden hair around one finger. "I am just keeping my peace about it right now. Who would I turn to? If I went to the inspector, he might dig too deep or read my diary for evidence, and then Sydney would be endangered. No, I will protect him and trust that he will clear his name and come for me in his time."

I wanted to shout that she was a sheltered girl of sixteen. That I had, not many months before, seen another young girl, lovely and full of life, refuse to take a risk seriously and pay for it before she had a chance to learn better.

But I merely took a deep breath and poured the tea.

"Well, then. What can I do about it, Ella? At least give me permission to watch your back."

She considered this a moment, stirring a lump of sugar into her tea very deliberately.

"You may watch my back. In a funny way, I think you intimidate people." She looked at me keenly. "People don't believe they can fool you."

Score one for the girl. At least she noticed that much.

Thirteen

The greatest enemy of the faerie-beast is the Prince of Faerie, for he will lay down his life in defense of another, and in that, a faerie-beast can never match him.

—A History of Faerie and the Folk

THE DAY of the Armentrout party held the last real storm of the season, one of those petty moments of late fall. The sky was nearly as dark as night a good three hours early, and thunder growled over the bay.

I did not wait to be fashionably late, but arrived as soon as I was able, hoping the storm would blow itself out while I was there and dissipate before I had to leave.

Senator Armentrout was standing in the doorway to greet his guests—I can guess that the only guests he really cared about were those inclined to vote, but I smiled and shook his hand anyway.

His hand felt like a cold fish.

"Welcome," he said, and his eyes passed on the guest behind me before I could so much as reply. So much for the importance of my vote.

"Miss Hanover."

It was Nicholas, standing in the hallway leaning on his cane.

"Nicholas! Oh, it is good to see you." I went over and took his hand in both of mine.

"And you. You're looking a little brighter, I think."

"One can hope," I answered cynically.

"This way." He started down the hall. "I have a quiet room where we can stay away from the rowdier set tonight. And from the storm. Ella is coming, and it will be a fine evening."

"You seem well prepared for the night."

"I should be. Father's had the household upended for this. He is displeased he will not be able to show off his gardens. But it was getting colder anyway. Half of the guests he cares about would catch cold this time of year."

I smothered a laugh.

"Speaking of, there goes the Shabby Lord," I said, raising my glass to point him out. The fellow was passing with his long-legged stride, bent with the weight of his medals.

"Whom?"

"Colonel Streatfield. The girls call him the Shabby Lord or the Wandering Prophet, since he's always harping about some cause or another."

"They should not make fun of him. He has seen more than most of them ever will."

"Well, he's hardly in vogue either. His opinions, his uniform—even his hair is decades out of fashion."

But Nicholas just shook his head.

"This society worships shallow things as if they can be obtained and held by sheer willpower. They dance on the edges of precipices, never dreaming their ruin could be inches—seconds—away. Any one of us could be. Our futures are little more than hopes."

We went into the room he'd set aside; it was comfortably furnished with many chairs and a table with drinks and food. Along one wall were windows that ran from ceiling to floor.

A flicker lit them and thunder crashed immediately on its heel. I started.

"Close one," Nicholas laughed. "We'll have plenty

of that tonight. Make yourself comfortable, I am going on the lookout."

I settled myself on one of the gold-and-white-stitched seats and stared out of the rain-glazed windows. There was, I suppose, a sort of prettiness to the rain. The way it made the world outside look like a painting, all the edges blurred and gentled, the colors muted.

"Oh, Constance, I hoped you'd come!" Ella rushed into the room and came straight over.

"How are your hands?"

"Much better." She held them out to show me. There were still red lines where the cuts had been, but they were greatly improved.

Leone followed behind her, but when I glanced at him, he averted his eyes. Last of all, the lawyer came and posted himself next to the doorway.

I would have asked why he still insisted on following Ella to every party even though she had another escort, but I knew the answer. He was here to keep an eye on Leone.

The lawyer took off his glasses and wiped them surreptitiously on his suit jacket.

"There is food," said Nicholas. "Please, do help yourselves. And you, sir." He gestured to the lawyer. It was the first time I'd seen anyone acknowledge him like a human being. "Help yourself to this spread, or go out to the main hall and enjoy whatever my father has there. Ella is among friends here."

The lawyer looked slowly at us all and then gave a thin smile.

"Thank you." To my surprise, he left the room.

We talked a while longer, during which Leone said he needed to ask the chauffeur to check the covering on his car. He disappeared for a few minutes, coming back damp.

Monique passed by the door. She was wearing a beautiful ruby dress with long tassels and carrying two glasses of champagne.

"Monique, why don't you join us?" I asked. I hadn't seen her more than a couple times since the night Hector shot Leone.

She turned, surprised to see me.

"Oh, love, I can't tonight." She gave an apologetic smile. "Next time?"

"Of course. Whatever you like." I waved her on and watched her head on towards the place where all the politicians were debating over their glasses of sherry.

I had never before seen her remotely interested in that corner of society.

The evening that followed was my favorite party of the year. We ate and talked and laughed, and though Leone still sat next to Ella, with one arm over the back of the sofa behind her, there was something easier in his manner. Perhaps with a small audience he was not so worried about making such a show of himself.

It grew late by the clock—half past ten. Not late, perhaps, for a wild party, but late enough for a quieter affair.

"Should we go?" asked Ella, when she noticed the time.

Leone went to the window and drew the curtain back a little, peering out. "It's still raining too hard."

Convenient for him.

"Are you sure?" asked Ella. "A little rain will not melt me."

"It is raining very hard. See for yourself."

From across the room, her lawyer cleared his throat.

"Miss Whittington, you might consider listening to the gentleman and accepting his verdict. I can see from here it will be almost impossible for the driver to see."

"You are right," agreed Ella reluctantly. "I must think of the driver."

"I could ask for tea to be brought in," offered Nicholas. "After all, it is growing cold outside. Something warm would fortify you for your drive home when it clears."

"It's a delightful night for it!" Ella clapped her hands. "Oh please, let's."

"If you're not too tired, Nicholas," I interjected. "I do not want to overstay our welcome, as you are the host."

"Not at all." He waved my courtesy away. "Tea and good conversation can hardly be bettered."

"Why don't you tell us a story?" asked Ella, once we were all settled with our hot drinks. "A frightening one that will make us clutch our cups and be glad to be indoors."

"A frightening one? I don't know many of those." He bit his lip as he thought. "Here it is. I shall tell you one of faerie-beasts, then."

Ella drew in her breath softly. "Is it true?"

"Who's to say?" Nicholas grinned. "Though it happened on a night much like this one."

Ella cupped her hands around her cup of tea and leaned forward. I caught Leone looking at her at that moment, and there was a half-hidden look of amusement on his face.

"There was once a faerie prince, beloved by his people, good and brave," Nicholas began.

"Is this the same prince as before?" Ella asked eagerly.

"Some say it was, some say it wasn't. Faerie princes are rather easily clumped together in stories."

"I suppose that's true."

"In any case, word came to the faerie kingdom that there was a faerie-beast roaming free, and he was not terrorizing one person, but many. As prince, it was his duty to go find the faerie-beast and stop it, even if it meant putting himself in harm's way. So the prince buckled on his sword, received the blessing of the king and queen on his venture, and went to the overworld, to the village where the reports had come from.

"It was not easy. When faerie-beasts come into our world, they do not bear the markings of a beast, but rather the heart of one. To find one, you must first force him to reveal himself. And that is a dangerous business."

"How does one do it?" Ella asked, breathless.

"A faerie-beast is unnaturally strong in the world of men. If you could challenge one to a task or show of strength, you might be able to catch them that way. The other way is harder and more dangerous. If you challenge one, declaring its true nature to its face, it will show its true colors for the space of a heartbeat."

"Why is that so dangerous?" asked Leone, with a laugh.

"Because you are staring a faerie-beast right in the

face, and you have just unmasked it. Nothing angers it more."

The laughter stilled on Leone's face.

"So," Nicholas continued, "the prince went to this village and entered during the day so that he might observe those in the town. There were women doing the washing at the fountain, there were tradesmen sitting outside their doors or just inside open windows, working at their trade, and flocks of healthy sheep being driven in to drink. It was a peaceful-seeming place. Not the sort of place you would suspect a faerie-beast to be hiding in. Though it is known that faerie-beasts will often target the brightest, happiest places and imitate the behaviors of those who live there, in order to ingratiate themselves before they destroy everyone."

Ella gave a little shiver.

"And so the prince came to the fountain and listened awhile to the women's conversation. They spoke of a girl who had disappeared, and another who had claimed to have run into the beast at night. And he asked the women for a drink, and when a young girl offered him water, he asked what household she was from. She was not anybody particular. Not remarkably beautiful or skilled or powerful. She was the third daughter of a merchant, the sort of man who had to travel often to make his living. His girls kept the sheep in the nearby meadows surrounding the town. But she invited him home, for he was dust-covered and worn and seemed, to her eyes, slight and underfed.

"He stayed with them for a week, observing the town, talking with the tradesmen, and making friends as best he could. But there was one man who could not stand the sight of him: a blacksmith who mocked him and called him a danger and stirred up the men of the town against him. And one night they brought torches to the house where he was staying and demanded that his hosts send him away or else give him up to them, for they were convinced he was a faerie-beast come in traveler's form.

"The merchant was away that night, and the third daughter, being the boldest, refused them entry. She begged the men of the town to hear her, but only two men would listen: a farmer, who had a daughter of his own the same age; and the tailor, a mild-faced man who sat on his stoop quietly and sewed every day. These two took her part and spoke for the stranger and turned the mob away, and in thanks, the girl invited them in for a bowl of milk. But the blacksmith, thwarted in his purpose, turned around and came back and found the prince returning to his bed in the stable above the sheep.

"'What quarrel do you have with me?' the prince asked the man. And the blacksmith replied that he had no quarrel with him, in truth, but that he wished to take away some of the sheep and the presence of a guest made it impossible. Then the prince knew that this man was a faerie-beast, for no true man would be so honest as to a dishonest purpose, but being in his presence, the beast could speak nothing but the truth, for he was the prince.

"The prince refused, as he must, and told the beast he had come to rid the town of him. And so he drew his sword, but as he did, the blacksmith struck him with a shepherd's crook leaned against the door, and the blow fell hard and shattered the prince's arm.

"And the faerie-beast told him again that he had no quarrel with him—that if he were to leave now, he would not pursue him nor hurt him further, and that he would only take of the sheep and be gone. But the prince had sworn an oath and he was not to be deterred. So they fought, and even with his arm broken, the prince overcame the faerie-beast at last by means of his skill. For faerie-beasts are strong, but the prince is always swift and quick with his sword.

"Weary and cradling his broken arm, he limped to the house for aid. But as he entered, he was met by the mother and the two older daughters. During the last half-hour, the third sister had disappeared, and so had the quiet tailor who had spoken for her. And they were worried, because it was not like her and a storm was blowing in. So the prince told them that he would find her, and they bound up his arm and he went his way. He found their footprints not far from the barn and tracked them into town. And there, as the rain began to pour, he found the second and canniest of the faerie-beasts.

"It was, after all, the quiet tailor who had done nothing but sew quietly on his stoop all day. And the beast smiled a grim smile and said with no fear at all, 'I am strongest among my brethren and I have sworn that I will, when I meet him, slay the Faerie Prince and cast his body across the entrance of Faerie. The overworld is my domain.' But the prince's courage rose. A beast might overcome him in this world, but he would not turn away in fear. 'Slay me if you must,' he swore, 'but I will not yield.' And so began one of the fiercest fights in all the history of Faerie.

"The beast was mighty, savage, and bloodthirsty, and he tore at the prince until he was bleeding and sorely wounded. Yet, the prince fought on, and at last wounded the faerie-beast sore also. And the faerie-beast spoke and said, 'Leave me the girl and I will leave you be. Bind up your wounds and live to fight another day.' For he knew that the greatest defeat the prince could take would be to yield up one he'd sworn to protect, and the prince was bloodied and swaying with weariness. But the prince rose up and said in a voice that could be heard over the rain, 'You will not touch her,' and flung himself at the beast. And the rain beat down upon them—upon the broad shoulders of the faerie-beast and upon the gentle face of the prince, so thickly that those watching in fear could not discern how the battle went. After a time, the sounds of the battle ceased, but no one could see through the rain and none dared go for fear that the beast was the victor. And then at last, through the rain-curtain, came the figure of the girl, dragging over her shoulder the wounded form of the prince—her champion.

"He was cared for by the town for two weeks as he recovered, and when he had left them, they planted a ring of snowdrops in the place where he had fought, in memory of his courage. And ever after, they have been the flower of the prince of faerie."

"Snowdrops," echoed Ella. "How lovely."

"I have always been fond of them myself," said Nicholas, his eyes warm. "They are beautiful."

"Do you think that faerie-beasts still roam, sometimes?"

"I imagine so," replied Nicholas. "They are wicked and cruel, but their deeds could be anything from murder to simple thievery. Some are not so dangerous as others, but all take advantage of the innocent and do wrong. Otherwise, they would not be beasts."

Near the window, the lawyer cleared his throat. "Miss Whittington, the rain has subsided. We should go."

Ella stood up with reluctance. "Well, go have the automobile brought around, won't you, and I will say my goodbyes."

She hugged Leone first, then me, and shook Nicholas's hand with great warmth.

For once, Leone did not leave at the same time she did, but lingered a few minutes longer in the doorway where I was observing the larger party from a comfortable distance.

"Are you going to speak to me, Miss Hanover, or simply ignore my existence from here on out?" He sounded almost penitent.

"I don't trust you," I replied. "You are dangerous, and destruction seems to follow in your wake."

There was silence between us as we regarded the party, the politicians, the raucous laughter, the hollow people going through the motions.

He looked down, flicking at his fingernail. "We're all vessels of destruction, my dear."

I turned in surprise to retort some answer, but he'd

already started to walk away, out towards the front entrance.

As my eyes were drawn back to the crowd, I saw a strange thing: the Shabby Lord was standing with one of the household staff, talking in a low voice. Then, quickly and quietly, he handed a small packet over to him. The man tucked it away into his coat and slipped out the other direction.

I watched, entranced, as the Shabby Lord strode back to the party, got his coat, and left, as simple and clean and unobserved as the wind in the trees outside.

Even the most upright seemed to have secrets. And right now, secrets were a dangerous commodity.

Fourteen

Faeries love mortals, mostly from afar, and sometimes laugh at their dreary ways, but there are times where the deeds of mortals are so wonderful that even the faeries must pause in their merrymaking and wonder.

—A History of Faerie and the Folk

I KEPT a close eye on everyone the next chance I got. It was a dance, and I did not expect to see many politicians in attendance.

And yet the Shabby Lord was there, his hands clasped behind his back philosophically, walking up and down on his long legs and talking earnestly to whoever would listen.

His cause again, no doubt.

"Now what might you be doing, Miss Hanover?" Leone's voice broke in on my thoughts. "Judging us all?"

"Observing." I glanced up at him. "Do you have a problem with that?"

He crooks one eyebrow.

"It depends on who you're watching, I suppose."

"Everyone." I did not want to tell him any of my suspicions; I didn't trust the man further than I could throw him. "I am watching you, you know."

"Aren't you afraid of telling me that? That I might do something about it?" He smiled, but there was a little glint in his eyes.

I pulled at the fingertips of my gloves casually. "No, not particularly." I was not going to be intimidated by this man.

"Suit yourself."

He moved away through the crowd, and shortly after I saw him dancing with Ella, who was wearing a beautiful silver dress.

I watched Colonel Streatfield in conversation with a portly old senator, one of the few others who had actually seen war.

The two suited each other.

They left the room together, going out into the hallway. As subtly as I could, I stole out in the same direction, making as if to pass by on an errand of my own.

As I stepped out into the hall, I saw it again—something changing hands furtively, a small envelope this time.

"Thank you." Streatfield shook the other man's hand warmly. He cleared his throat and adjusted his spectacles.

"Evening—Miss Hanover, is it?"

"It is."

I hadn't mean to be caught in conversation with him, but I wasn't going to shy away from it either. One can often discern a lot about a person just after a surreptitious act, if one knows how to look for the signs.

"I know your father a little."

"Ah." I laughed. "A good thing or a bad thing?"

"Good, mostly," he replied, looking me in the eye. "You know, he loved polo when he was young. We used to play each other."

I tried to envision that. Nowadays the colonel would look like a scarecrow on a horse and my father a ruffled pigeon.

"It must have been a long time ago," I replied, with a straight face.

"Long enough. Tell your father hello from me when you see him."

"I will."

He had not exhibited a single sign of nervousness, save clearing his throat loudly, which he always did.

But I knew what I had seen, and I was not to be put off.

I found the Wolf-Catcher in one corner of the ballroom, looking more like he wasn't enjoying himself than usual.

I went to him and stood close enough that I didn't have to shout. "Inspector? May I speak to you for a moment?"

He looked surprised that I should be coming to him for anything but a sarcastic comment.

"Of course." He sniffed and straightened his shoulders. "Come this way, where it is quieter."

His demeanor was more official now than it had been a moment ago. Standing, watching the dancing, he was a man on reluctant duty. Now he was a man preparing himself to deal with a problem.

When we'd gained a small, private room, he turned to me. "Now, what is it?"

"I have seen Colonel Streatfield passing small

envelopes and parcels at parties, twice now in the last week. His manner was—secretive."

"You think he's taking bribes?"

"Or giving them. I don't know. Maybe something worse. I do know that something is not right this season. I've seen and heard too many strange things."

"In that you are correct," replied Rothschild with a sad smile. "But the colonel is not a man I can easily see being involved in shady dealings. We may differ in our political convictions, but his character has always been impeccable."

"But you'll look into it?"

He had pulled a notebook from his breast pocket and was scribbling something with the nub of a pencil.

"Yes, I will."

He snapped the notebook shut and pocketed it.

The music had grown noisy and the dancing wild, and I stepped into it with a sudden, strange feeling of being somewhere I'd been before, but as a different person.

Before, the quick running beat had flowed over me like a river over a stone. The more alive the music had been, the more it made me feel dead inside.

It felt different now. It still had no real taste to me, but it felt like music. I could see how someone might be swept up in it and fall in love, or feel their pain disappear for a little while.

Marge loved music like this. She'd put it on the gramophone and turn it up as far as it would go. It would annoy Mother and fluster Father and she'd just laugh.

I resented her because we both knew better and she did it anyway. Some days I wished I could just break out the way she did.

And now here I was, standing in the doorway in my black-and-gold dress, listening to the music. Caught between my old life and something that felt new.

I felt as if perhaps, when I left the doorway, I could leave it a different person. It was the strangest feeling, and I didn't know if I liked it.

Ella was talking to someone at the edge of the dance floor, wearing her usual smiling, earnest expression. But Leone's face was taut.

Something was wrong.

Quietly, he reached his hand out and caught her fingertips with his. She excused herself with a smile and followed him out, past me, into the hall from which I had come.

The music continued to roar on for the next few minutes—Marge's favorite song, one of my least favorites.

Mercifully, I knew when it would end. There was a brief lull as the musicians changed their sheet music.

And that's when I heard a voice, low and in distress.

I went down the hall towards the first doorway and stopped short. I had narrow line of sight through the door and into the room.

It was Ella.

She was crying silently now, her eyes full of tears. Leone was leaning forward earnestly, one hand on her shoulder.

"You don't need to come back to this place, not ever, if you do not want," he whispered. "Do you hear me?"

She nodded.

"Oh, Ella." He leaned close, his lips nearly brushing her hair. "This is no place for a girl like you."

She looked up at him, straight and direct. "Then please, take me away."

"I will," he said, wrapping her in his arms. "I will."

He rested his chin on her head, and only I caught the slow smile he smiled to himself.

I did not see them again that night.

Leone was strangely absent from the next gathering, and Ella was there, her usual cheery self. The distraught Ella I had seen at the last party was nowhere to be found.

Albert Rothschild sought me out on his own, just as I was leaving the smoking parlor. There was a certain gleam in his eye as if he'd been amused by something.

"Miss Hanover?" he greeted. "I have looked into your concerns quite thoroughly, and I am pleased to tell you that you have no reason for concern."

"But I saw him pass a packet to one of Senator Armentrout's staff at the party," I insisted. "His manner was very secretive, I assure you."

"I don't doubt that, but not every secret is a bad one, Miss Hanover."

"But—" I couldn't continue. It was a strange sense more than a fact, but so many people had been odd that night. It had all felt so connected.

He motioned me over. "I will set your mind at ease, if you like, provided you keep this in confidence."

"Of course."

I leaned close and he lowered his voice.

"The colonel supports a number of men from his regiment who are unable to work because of their service. Some with large families." A twinkle came into his eye. "He does it—anonymously."

"Oh."

His eyes light with amusement at the surprise on my face. "Does that satisfy you?"

"I suppose it must," I replied, strangely forlorn.

"Don't worry, Miss Hanover. Take heart that you are an observant young woman and that there is still some integrity in this world. Heaven knows we could use more of it."

He winked, actually winked, and took a sip of his champagne.

Wonders never cease.

I wandered over the side of the house where the political men smoked and drank their sherries.

In this house, it was a wide room, almost the size of the ballroom, and there was quite a selection today. Nicholas's father was among them, voicing some opinion loudly.

The Shabby Lord was there, his hands thrust into his pockets, his gray shoulders slumped a little, no medals on his chest.

He was not in full dress uniform tonight.

I suppose I should not have been so quick to be cynical. A reputation was still worth something, it seemed, in this cheap world.

He stood talking calmly, another trait he did not share with most of his colleagues. His thick gray hair was still decidedly out of style, but looking at him today, it didn't seem to make a difference.

He was distinguished in my mind in a way he had never been before.

There was a tenacity in his manner that you had to respect. No matter what anyone else thought about him or said behind their hands, he knew he had nothing to be ashamed of. He could not have cared less what people said about him, so long as he knew he was in the right.

To go about as he did, tirelessly looking for support for his good causes, was one thing. But to privately use his money to make a better life for those who couldn't make one for themselves, gaining no recognition for it, was another thing entirely.

And dusty and old-fashioned as he was, in that moment I thought I might give anything to have what he had.

Fifteen

It is said that in time of need, the Faerie Prince can cast a glamor over himself, making him unrecognizable for a time to those around him, so that he might walk unseen among his enemies and rescue his own.

—A History of Faerie and the Folk

"Constance, do you have a favorite flower?" Ella was bent over the last of the season's daisies.

"I can't say I've thought much about it."

"Could you hand me the scissors?"

I handed the scissors over.

"Daisies are mine." She pull a handful into the basket I was holding. "Ever since I was little."

"Why is that?"

"Because they are so beautiful and white and they thrive anywhere. It's said that the Queen of the Faeries loves them."

"How is it that you know so much about Faerie? Every time I turn around you are either reading about it or talking about it."

"I read books about it when I was a girl and never stopped loving it," she said. "Doesn't it give you a sense of wonder to think that there could be places of untold beauty just moments away, if only you knew where to look for them?"

I shrugged. I had never been the one with a taste for such things.

But her face was so bright, so sweet, that I added, "What do you love about it the most?"

She thought about this a moment.

"Faerie is supposed to be very beautiful," she said thoughtfully, "but I think what I love most is how the people of Faerie spread beauty and do not live for themselves. How the Faerie Prince can glamor himself and walk among common folk, and it wearies him, but he does it to find the lost and bring them home. And the queen, she spreads beauty wherever she goes, be it flowers or snow...."

The sound of an automobile came from around the house, and Prince, laying on the veranda, started up with a bark.

A minute later, Leone came around the side of the house, playing with Prince, trying to prise his ball from of his mouth.

"I wonder what he is here for." Ella straightened, looking towards the pair with a small furrow between her brows.

"You're not expecting him?"

"He doesn't need to be expected," she answered with a little smile.

"Apparently not."

"Ladies!" He lifted one hand and waved.

"Hello!" Ella waved back and motioned him over. "We're just picking the last of the flowers."

"The first and the last are always the sweetest," he replied, with a nod to me and a kiss on the cheek for Ella.

Ella picked one of the daisies out of the basket and handed it to him. "The last ones are bittersweet."

He sniffed it and poked it into his buttonhole.

"We'll have to order flowers for your party, sadly. It will be too cold then."

"You're having a party?" I had not heard this.

"Yes. At the end of the month. I thought it was time I threw one."

"I wish you could have thrown a summer party, you know." Leone was surveying the garden with a thoughtful air, "That golden hair of yours would have been beautiful in a daisy crown."

"I don't need to wear a daisy crown in front of everyone to enjoy it," she laughed, tucking a couple into her hair. "What do you think?"

"My queen." He caught her hand and kissed it.

Ella giggled.

"You must have a few on the night of your party. Even if you hide them in a secret parlor where the politicians can't see."

"I don't care if they see." She wrinkled her nose. "They could use a little cheer in their lives, most of them."

"Miss Hanover, what do you think? About those poor politicians?" There was teasing in his voice.

"They have far too much money and power for the amount of time they spend smoking cigars," I replied. "Perhaps they are cheerless, but they've brought it on themselves."

"Oh!" Leone laughed. "The girl doesn't mince her words."

"I have never minced them. You should know that by now."

"I stand chastened." He gave a little bow.

"You still haven't told me why you came," said Ella.

"Do I need a reason?" he teased.

"Last time you said you missed me, but we'd seen each other just that morning. I am starting to expect more."

"I wanted to see how you were," he said simply.

"I'm all right," she said, a little pointedly.

"Good. Then I suppose my work here is done."

"You aren't staying?"

"I shouldn't," said Leone regretfully. "I just wanted to see how you were. Go ahead, I'll play with Prince while you put those in water. You can come say goodbye in a few minutes."

"All right," Ella sighed. "Come on, Constance. I'll ask them to put some tea together."

But as we headed up the steps to the terrace, Ella cast a sad glance over her shoulder in his direction.

"Why do you like Leone so much?" I asked. "You say he makes you laugh, but he also seems to make you sad sometimes."

"Love is complicated," said Ella. "But I suppose you know that."

"Yes."

"When you love someone, you worry for them sometimes more than you enjoy their presence. And there have been some worrisome things."

"With him?"

"Not him personally."

She forced a smile onto her face as we passed a servant, just inside the doorway. "Could you have the kitchen put together some tea?" When the servant had gone, she turned to me. "Hold these, will you? I will get a vase."

She left the room and I was left standing alone, holding a basket of flowers. A maid passed through the room and paused at the window.

"I do not trust that man," she said, shaking her graying head.

"Who, Mr. Leone?"

"The same. Suspicious character."

"I don't disagree, but do you have a reason?"

"Well," she pursed her lips and closed the curtain. "He has the look of trouble, for one thing. Don't tell me you don't see it in his eyes and in the way he smiles. It's the way he took such a quick shine to Miss Ella, and the fact that he sneaks around here but never comes inside. Why should he avoid us?"

"Perhaps he finds the house dull with no one else in it."

"He finds Miss Ella diverting enough," she replied brusquely. "And he was in the house the day Mr. Whittington died."

"What?" The world seemed to stop.

"The day Mr. Whittington died—it was the first day I saw that boy. He was upstairs."

"You're sure about that? Him?"

"As sure as I can be. There were comings and goings that day, but I saw that young man duck into one of the rooms as I was coming upstairs. I remembered because it was one of the rooms we don't use anymore, not since Mrs. Whittington left us."

"You told the police this?"

"I told the lawyer. He knows all the policies and the protocol, and Miss Ella's welfare is his business. If there was something amiss, he'd report it."

"Hm."

I looked out the window as Ella and Leone said goodbye. The laughter, the talking that they couldn't quite bring themselves to end, the way he bent down to kiss her cheek.

I'd have thought a man like Leone would press his advantage more, but perhaps Ella's innocence made him treat her a little differently.

He got into his automobile and roared off.

"Sorry it took awhile," said Ella coming in. "I did find a vase."

She set it down on the table.

The maid had left while I was observing their good-byes, and in the privacy of the empty room, I told Ella what the woman had said.

"Impossible." She shook her head. "He never came around here until after we met at the party. We've talked of it many times."

"What if he's lying to you?"

"He's not."

She turned her focus to the flowers, seemingly unconcerned. Humming under her breath, she began to arrange them.

"You see, I am going abroad." She did not look at me when she said it.

A bad feeling started in me. "Abroad? When?"

"After the end of the month. Right after my party—it's kind of a going away affair."

"For how long?"

She shrugged. "As long as I like. I spent so much of my life here—all of it, actually. I have the means, and I think it is time to see something of the world."

"I agree that seeing the world sounds wonderful," I said. "But I think it puts you in a dangerous position, don't you?"

"Dangerous?"

"You're so young, Ella. You are a target for people who can smell a fortune a mile away. Here, it's bad, with people fawning over you, but out there—it will be twice that. Who are you going abroad with?"

"What do you mean?"

"You know what I mean."

"It doesn't matter. Myself."

"Ella! Listen to sense."

"Why do you care so much? I'm not in any more danger abroad than here."

"I care because you are innocent and trusting and exactly the sort of person thieves and swindlers look for. You have a few of them following you around as it is."

"I hope you aren't talking about Leone."

I laughed, hard. "He's the picture of a swindler, and you just let him right in. Welcomed him with open arms."

"Constance, he's not."

"Not? What does it say when a man swaggers in on one woman's arm and changes his affections within a week? Or when he spends all his time with you, without giving you any kind of understanding?"

"He loves me," Ella protested.

"Has he spoken to you of commitment? Does he have

means of his own? Ella, this is exactly what swindlers do. They use charm and good looks to worm their way into circles with money, and they find the most likely person to take advantage of, and that, Ella, is you, if only because of your age and your recent introduction to society."

"He's not going to take advantage of me. He promised."

"He promised?"

I laughed again. Could she really be this naive?

"What does your lawyer have to say about him?"

"He's not fond of him," she admitted, "but he's only jealous. He doesn't like me having someone else to listen to."

"Or he's protective, because that's what a lawyer is for."

"I don't like Mr. Simmonds."

"Of course you don't. He's middle-aged and stuffy and tells you things you don't want to hear. Ella, I have no interest in this matter besides your safety, and I need you to listen to me."

She looked at me, her lips pressed together. I had her ear, but not her heart.

"I overheard you at the Emmersons' ball, when Leone told you that he'd take you away."

Her face went strangely blank.

"Sometimes people hear things and misunderstand them," she said.

"Did I misunderstand this?"

"Yes," she replied. "A little."

"Which part did I misunderstand?"

"I was tired of people and I wanted to go home," she answered stubbornly. "He told me he would take me."

I let out my breath slowly. It was a reasonable enough explanation, as the Emmersons and anyone closely associated with them were, as a rule, jaded and rude, and no one could be blamed for wanting to exit their company. But I'd seen the way Leone and Ella talked that night, and it was nothing like asking for a ride home after a party gone sour.

It was more than that.

"Ella, can you promise me you are not running away with Leone?"

"No, because you cannot force me to promise things."

"Ella, what do I have to say to you to convince you that Leone does not love you and does not mean you well? He wants your money. He knows how to make an entrance, he plays his cards like a master. The only people with cause to do that are ones hiding intentions other than those they profess."

Her face looked as wounded as if I'd called her

grandmother's honor into question, and I lost my patience.

All I had wanted was to help, and look where it got me. I stormed out of the house and shut the door hard after myself.

As I drove home, I remembered—strange, how my mind had put it away until now—that Marge and I had had a fight one of the last times we'd ever talked.

The fight was not out of the ordinary, probably one of the reasons I hadn't given it a thought. But it had been the last time we'd really looked each other in the eye, the last time she'd worn her favorite dress, the long, slim one with the loose green fringe.

She'd taken a dress of mine without asking, ripped it above the hem, and then lied about it. I'd taken the dress downstairs to the front hall (the only place I seemed to be able to find her those days, coming in and out) and showed it to her.

"Interesting. You tore your dress," she'd said, breezily.

"I haven't worn this dress in months," I replied. "And I saw you sneaking out of my room the other night."

"If you haven't worn it, why do you care?"

"Because it belongs to me, and unlike you, I care for

my things. I am not careless and wasteful enough to ruin a dress the first time I wear it."

"That wasn't me."

"No one else would have worn it, Marge, and you know that."

"I didn't wear it," she replied, with a little smile. "Agnes did."

"Agnes ripped it?" Agnes was one of Marge's favorite friends and one of my least favorite. Take every silly thing a girl could be—and say—and that was Agnes.

"I guess. She's always catching her trains in the doors of automobiles and ripping them. It's a dreadful habit."

"You gave Agnes my dress?"

"Well, she hadn't anything smart to wear."

"Next time Agnes wants to be a leech, you let her leech off you like a true friend. What kind of friend only sacrifices someone else's things?"

She'd snatched the dress out of my hand and thrown it on the floor.

"You are nothing but a child!" I'd shouted at her. "Get out of here, I don't ever want to see you again!"

"Well, if that's how you want to treat your sister, you go ahead." She breezed out, slamming the door after her.

I remember wishing she'd trip on her ridiculous heels and break her neck on the way out.

I only saw her once after that. A brief conversation two days later, the afternoon before she died.

I am sure the fight didn't help my state of mind two days later when the news came of her death. She'd gotten away with being reckless and foolish for a long time, and in a way, I'd rather expected something to go wrong. Just nothing so permanent.

I just couldn't bring myself to let her get away with it all so easily.

I slammed the car door when I got home, stalked into the house.

There was something wrong about all of this. I didn't know why I cared so much, why I was so angry at Ella, or why it made me think of Marge.

But as I stepped into the house, I realized the frustration was the same—I wanted someone to see something I saw, and they wouldn't.

It was Leone, all these little pieces coming at me fast and broken, the way the light from the headlamps of an automobile is fractured as it passes tree after tree.

He had Ella's ear. He talked smoothly, he knew her plans. If he wanted, he could kidnap her after the party, and everyone would simply think she'd gone abroad. No one would be the wiser.

Sixteen

*To understand the ways of Faerie, one must see past the
fleetingness of the grand things and see how rather, it is
the ordinary and simple things that endure.*

—A History of Faerie and the Folk

I CALLED Ella the next day to apologize. I had not
changed my mind about the wisdom of her plans, nor I
was a whit less suspicious. But if I was to convince her—
and especially if I could not—I must not let this friendship go to ruin now.

"I was thinking of calling you too," Ella said softly,

when I had apologized. "I didn't want it to come between us. I promise, I'll watch myself carefully."

"You don't have to make up your mind now," I said.

"I suppose," she said. "But I already know what I want to do, deep down. I am ready to go. And I would rather not give you false hope."

I just stared out the window at the mostly bare trees, heaving and bowing under the strong wind.

"Constance? Are you there?"

"I'm here."

"I hope you aren't angry."

"No." But worried. And I had no idea how I was going to bring the danger of her situation across to her.

"Don't worry about me, Constance. You have done so much for me already."

"Having done does nothing for future concern."

"I know." Her voice had a touch of understanding.

There was a silence on the line.

"Look," I said at last, "at least tell me that you will come for dinner before you leave. I'll invite some friends. It will be quiet."

"Oh Constance, that would be lovely."

"Thursday next?"

"Yes."

"I will plan on it."

. . .

The following Thursday came soon enough. There were few parties left this season; the election was over and the weather had turned, and it wasn't quite cold enough yet for winter festivities.

I chose a camel-colored dress for the dinner party. I had just come downstairs and paused before the mirror in the front hall to make sure my hair was just so, when my mother appeared from the front room.

"Where are you going, Constance?"

"Nowhere. I am having a dinner party, remember?"

"Ah, yes." My mother paused and stared at me closely. "But you don't look well, Constance. Not at all."

"Just tired."

"Mind you go to fewer parties, then. They keep you up late."

"I've been going to fewer," I told her. "Really. I don't think that's the cause."

"The dinner?"

"No. That isn't any trouble. But I've been doing a lot of thinking and worrying, and I've found it can be very tiring."

Something like understanding crossed her usually proud, stern face. "Poor dear. It can be. Take some veronal tonight and see if that helps."

"Thanks, Mother."

"Are you using the Denver plates?"

"Yes."

"Good. They're the best for entertaining." She patted my hand as if she was proud of me.

A small piece of me was pleased. Not that I cared overly for entertaining, or even her opinion, but there was something peaceful about her approval of me. It made me feel that perhaps there was a way forward out of this. Out of our strife and boredom and distance from one another.

Nicholas was the first to arrive, polite and on time.

"Nicholas, how are you?" I asked he stepped in and shed his coat, handing it to a waiting servant.

"Never been better," he smiled, switching his cane to his left hand so as to shake mine. "And you?"

"I am as you see," I replied wryly. I was not sure myself.

Ella and Leone came together, fashionably late and for once not shadowed by her lawyer.

"Did you ask Mr. Simmonds to stay behind?" I asked Ella softly.

"No, he just didn't come out of his office when I went to leave. I suppose he has a lot of work, what with my going away and all. Leone drove me, anyhow. I gave my chauffeur the night off."

"Enjoying the time you have left together?" I asked slyly.

"Leone has been busy," said Ella, a little sadly. "We've only talked while in the automobile this week."

"We'll make up for it tonight," he said, squeezing her hand in his.

Dinner was a quiet, pleasant affair, as I had promised. With just the four of us, the conversation was comfortable—at least on the surface—and we lingered around the table with our after-dinner coffee and continued to talk.

I was never given to sentimentality, but in that moment when Nicholas looked up at the servant with a smile to thank them for bringing the coffee and Ella leaned forward to admire the way the light fell over the tablecloth, I thought that perhaps this was the moment the whole season was leading up to. All the weary watching and going out to try to spark a flame that had died—it had brought me to this quiet, good moment with people I truly cared about.

And Leone.

I looked over at him and noted nothing possessive in his manner, though I looked for it. His large hand was resting in Ella's with a kind of acquiescence, letting her hold his hand captive as if it made her feel safe.

I wished she wouldn't.

"I cannot believe this time is ending so quickly," said Ella. "All my life, I moved almost outside of time. Now the weeks race by faster than a train. It makes me feel like my life will be over in no time at all."

"Nonsense, you have so much life ahead of you," I said. "This is only the beginning."

"But that's the thing," Nicholas said with a philosophical air, toying with his cuff. "We don't actually know what time we have. It's all a guess, based on past experience, current health, and particular hopes. We don't have a promise that any one of us will take our next breath."

"What a drab thought," said Leone, but his heart did not seem quite in it tonight. "I'd rather just think like I will live forever, and let it be a surprise."

And at that moment I remembered something that Marge said once, when we were very young.

"Constance," she'd said, when we'd put our dolls away in their beds for the night and said their prayers for them. "When I die, I hope I don't know."

"What do you mean?"

"Like the dolls, if they die before they wake. I'd like to just think I was going to sleep or fainting. Wouldn't that be best?"

"I'd rather know," I'd replied.

"Well, I wouldn't." She pushed her hair out of her face philosophically. "I hope I go while I'm laughing."

And she climbed into bed, and we said no more about it.

"Constance?" Ella leaned across the table. "Are you all right?"

"Perfectly." I recovered myself quickly. "Just thinking."

"What are your thoughts?" asked Nicholas.

I looked from Nicholas to Leone and didn't answer right away. I poured a cup of coffee out, stirred cream into it, took a sip as I thought.

"I don't know, to be frank. I expect I fall somewhere near the belief that life isn't easy and we die anyway, so why bother too much about anything?"

"That's not what I would have expected," said Leone.

"Really? What would you have expected?"

"Not sure." He stroked his smooth chin. "Something a little closer to hedonism. But not so far as 'eat, drink, and be merry, for tomorrow we die.'"

"That was my sister Marge," I said. "And she got exactly what she believed—only I don't think she ever thought it would happen to her."

"Most don't," said Leone, shaking his head in what appeared to me false remorse.

"Including you, I think."

"What, me?" His voice was surprised, but he was grinning. "If the shoe fits, I must wear it, I suppose."

"What do you think of that, Nicholas?" asked Ella.

Nicholas was taking a sip when the question was posed. He slowly swirled the last of the coffee in the bottom of his cup and set it down, studying it.

"I think," he replied, taking his time, "that when it comes down to it, we all agree that no one knows when death will come. And because of that, I think one should live in a manner they would not be ashamed of if they had to go the next day. And one should be kind, because they do not know if maybe it is their brother who goes soon."

A hot prickle ran over my shoulders. I knew he was not talking about me. It was, like everything else for him, a carefully considered comment. And a wise one, I'll allow.

But it felt as strong and direct as if we'd been the only two in the room.

"Nicholas," said Leone, "for a virtuous man like you, this sounds easy enough. But what about those of us who find it so very hard to be good?"

Nicholas chuckled softly.

"A thousand small decisions lead the big ones, my friend, and you know that well."

Leone laughed in a wry, chastened sort of way and poured himself more coffee.

I could not help feeling the difference in him tonight. Below the surface he was not quite himself. Preoccupied, perhaps.

After they left, I couldn't shake our conversation.

Before Marge died, I didn't think much about the length of life. Children died on occasion of accidents and fevers, and older members of society passed on. Funerals were a part of life, but not a part that mattered. Every few years, you try to feel sad for an hour in a cold room and then happily resume whatever it was that you were doing before.

The young men of our acquaintance talked about death in bold, boasting words, but the concept seemed as empty as the rest of what they said.

And then Marge died, and I understood that things aren't as certain as we think.

But what I wanted to do with my life, with what I had, had not become any clearer. I felt only dead and uninterested, even though Marge had not affected my life much, except to make it worse.

All these musings swarmed in my head as I changed out of my dress and readied myself for bed.

I went to my room and sat down on my bed and began to brush my hair.

We imagine there will be time when we are old to be good. It is a lie. Marge will never be old. Life is, as the poets say, fleeting. We don't really know the future, though we imagine we do.

Nicholas was more than content with his "living in a manner one will not be ashamed of," but as Leone had said, not all of us find it so easy.

Yet perhaps it isn't ever easy. Only men like Nicholas make it seem that way. Perhaps it is a struggle no matter who you are.

As I turned out the light and pulled the covers up over my shoulders, one last memory of Marge came to me.

She loved to say, "We don't wait. We live now," when she wanted to do something wild.

Perhaps she just had what living meant a bit upside down; she was talking about spending frivolously and speeding in her automobile, and life has to do with something harder and more lasting. But I think she was right.

We don't wait. We live now.

$$Seventeen$$

*There is no greater deed in the kingdom of Faerie than to
defend the life of the Queen with one's own.*

—A History of Faerie and the Folk

THE WHITTINGTON MANSION WAS ALIVE, blazing
with light. Cars lined the drive, headlamps cutting
through the late autumn darkness, leading the way like a
string of Christmas lights to the bright dwelling beyond.

It was, I had to admit, one of the most brilliant sights
I had seen all season long. Gone was the dusty air of old
mystery. The reign of Queen Ella had begun, and in
such a fashion. I'd nearly asked the chauffeur to drive

tonight, my mind was so full of other worries and preoccupations, but in the end, I liked the feel of my hands on the wheel and I didn't know if there was much else I would be able to control tonight.

I alighted at the steps, joining a dozen others ascending at the same time, women with thick wraps over glittering dresses that matched extravagant headbands. They were laughing, talking loudly already in the cold air that seemed to catch and hold their voices a moment before letting them fly up to the dark, cloudy sky.

I glanced up; I rather wished there had been stars.

The house opened bright, wide arms to receive me. I was enveloped in the rush. This was certainly more of a crowd than I'd seen at any party for the last two months. Music was already coming loudly from the ballroom, I could hear the clinking of glasses somewhere deeper in the throng, and the merry voices were a thick hum that drowned out nearly all else.

Ella met me near the doorway, wearing a beautiful black dress and a thick diamond necklace. Her thick golden hair was piled high on her head.

"Darling, you look ravishing," I said.

"Oh, thank you!" Her face lit up as bright as the diamonds. "You look beautiful too."

I'd worn black, too—a simple dress with a long string

of pearls. I had no need to make an impression on anyone.

"Where is Leone?" I had noticed his absence from her side immediately.

"Locking Prince away in one of the upstairs rooms." She took my hands and looked me in the eyes earnestly. "The poor boy gets lonely, you'll look in on him, won't you?"

"If Leone deigns to tell me which room it is."

"It's the only room along the upstairs balcony with an ivory handle, you can't miss it." She leaned over and gave me a kiss. "Here is a letter from me, but don't read it right away. It's a goodbye, and I didn't want to forget to give it to you. I'll be sure to find you a little later. I will escape my hostess duties for a few moments, at least."

"To be sure."

I moved on into the swollen river of people and left her to greet the next guest. I found Monique in the rush.

"Oh, Constance! I am ever so glad to see you!" She caught my arm in hers. "It has been so long."

"Yes." I agreed, having nothing else to say about it. It was strange that she should suddenly be so very chummy.

"It's awfully crowded," she murmured, her eyes roaming over the crowd. "Have you seen Leone yet?"

"No. Ella said he was upstairs."

"Oh."

"Why do you ask?"

"No reason," she answered rather quickly. The color was high in her cheeks tonight.

"We should find a quiet spot," I advised.

I found an inlet before the ballroom, a sort of side hallway that had a very long table and some ancient-looking paintings on the wall, and I pulled her in with me.

And there, of all people, was the Police Inspector Albert Rothschild, standing in the corner, his untouched champagne in his hand.

Monique went to the table to get a drink from the punch bowl, and I went over to the inspector, picking up a glass on the way by.

"I am surprised to see you here," I said. "Seeing as all the rumors have you extremely busy."

"Who says I am not?" He raised an eyebrow.

"In that case, may I conclude that you know something we do not?"

"That would be telling, wouldn't it?"

"I have no horse in the race, you know that."

He laughed, just a small thing through his nose. Then he glanced at Monique, still by the punch bowl, and leaned a little closer. "I am going to close the trap tonight."

"Here?"

"Yes, here."

He puts his finger to his lips.

So Sydney was to be here tonight. I suppose if all the stories were true, he could come by way of a secret passage. But why would he show himself tonight?

Unless Ella was in immediate danger.

"You're sure about this?" I pressed.

He just smiled, calm and assured. "I am."

I swallowed and shoved my thoughts deep down below my usual, couldn't-care-less mask.

"Then good luck to you, sir." I clinked my glass to his. "I am off to pleasure, and will leave you to your business."

I caught up Monique's arm again. "Come, darling, shall we see what else there is to try?"

She came along willingly. There was definitely something not right with her tonight.

We sampled the food, for which she had no appetite, but she was patient as I tried things, browsing over the hors d'oeuvres.

Her glass of punch was untouched too.

She kept looking through the crowd, but with interest in no one. Her face was starting to look wan under her makeup.

"What is the matter?"

"I am not feeling well," she murmured faintly.

"Come, let's find a place where you can rest." I led her away from the noise and down the hall to a study that looked clean but unused.

"Sit down," I urged, bringing her a chair and taking her punch glass out of her fingers.

"Thank you," she whispered, collapsing into the chair.

"What is the matter, do you know why you feel so ill?"

"I just have such an awful headache."

"I will get you an aspirin and a glass of water. And perhaps I should have your car brought round?"

"No, please don't leave."

"I'll only be a minute." I hesitated, already at the door.

"You will be quick?"

"Very."

"All right, then. Just close the door when you leave."

I stepped out into the hall and closed the door, waiting to feel it click shut.

The hall was quieter down here and I did not need to push through people as I had earlier. I passed a couple of young men trying their best to win over a pair of skeptical girls, and then I passed Simmonds the lawyer, looking strangely alone without Ella.

He paused as I passed.

"You've been with her," he said.

"Pardon?"

He leaned close as if to ask a further question, but then his eyes glanced over my shoulder. "Excuse me."

He gave his bland smile again and headed down the hall.

It did not take me long to find a member of the staff and make the request, and I was heading back to Monique's room with her water and aspirin no more than three or four minutes after leaving her.

I turned the knob and heard a man's voice.

"I thought you would have been smarter than this," the voice said as I pushed the door open. "That you would have listened to my first warning."

It was the lawyer.

Monique was standing against the wall, her face taut with fear, her hands pressed against the wallpaper, and the lawyer stood in front of her, close but not too close, as a dog might back someone into a corner.

He tsked very softly. "I wouldn't have thought it of a girl like you."

"And what do you think a 'girl like me' is?" whispered Monique, her voice trembling. "How do you know it's me?"

"It's taken me a long time," said the lawyer gently, so

very gently, and he reached out and put his hand on Monique's shoulder. "But I finally know it was you."

Monique froze.

I stepped in. "Excuse me, Mr. Simmonds, I think you must have the wrong person. Monique hasn't been—"

He turned and looked at me, and his face was so ordinary and unremarkable that it made the glint in his eyes stand out like a light in a forest.

"Miss De Flores?" He raised his eyebrows and looked over at her. "Do you have anything to say?"

She was white as a sheet and only shook her head.

"What Miss De Flores is afraid to say is that she has been spying for Sydney Whittington."

"Monique?"

"I can smell it on her," he sneered. "She reeks of him, she reeks of deception. And to think, all this time, this whole season you passed yourself off as a shallow, silly girl."

He reached out and seized her arm.

"Constance!" she called.

"Take your hands off her this moment." I grabbed his arm and he shook my hand off like nothing. The muscles beneath the sleeve were like iron, far too strong to be natural.

Our eyes met. His burned with cold anger.

For the briefest moment, we stood that way, eyes locked. His disdain was entirely unmasked, his lip curling in a sneer. He expected me to be frightened of him. He expected me to shrink back from him, trembling like Monique.

And he wasn't going to get away with that.

"You are a faerie-beast," I said, slow and deliberate, to his face. And I smiled.

His face turned truly horrible, like a curtain had been pulled away. It was still his face, but there was a wild, wolfish look in it. One ear, I swear, was pointed at the tip. His face twisted with anger, blue eyes burning with rage.

"You will be sorry you ever intervened," he hissed through clenched teeth.

"Monique, run."

She whirled and took off. Completely heedless of propriety, I ran after her. I felt the tips of the lawyer's fingers brush my shoulder, barely missing me.

I slammed the door behind us and ran down the hall.

"Don't look back, Monique!" I shouted. "Keep running!"

To my surprise, the door behind us did not open.

There are stories about this house. A dozen secret rooms and passageways, some leading even to Faerie.

"Keep running!"

We were in the one house he knew intimately. And I'd just made him terribly angry.

The hallway seemed to stretch before us forever, not another human in sight, no sound but the pounding of our feet and our own breathing.

Monique tripped on her heels and fell headlong with a shriek.

"Come on, you have to get up." My heart was pounding in my ears so hard it sounded like thudding footsteps surrounding us, coming for us. She was frantically pulling at her shoes, trying to get them off.

I grabbed her arm and dragged her to her feet.

We made it to the room at the end of the hall, a parlor near the front of the house. I dashed through the doorway and straight into Nicholas Armentrout.

He caught me in his arms, staggering backwards. "Constance, what is this?"

"Nicholas, please, there's someone after us."

"Who?"

"A—" The strangeness of it caught in my throat for a second. And then I realized he was the one ally we had. "A faerie-beast."

He didn't question. "Get behind me."

"Who are you?" asked Monique. Her hair was disheveled and her makeup smeared. I'd never seen her in such a state—she was always the image of perfection.

"Nicholas Armentrout," he glanced back with a brief smile. "The senator's son."

"I—don't think I've met you," she whispered, breathless. She looked about ready to collapse.

"Many haven't." He looked to me. "Constance, get that poker, will you?"

I ran to the fireplace and snatched it up.

"Watch the chimney, just in case. This house has secrets." He nodded at the poker in my hand. "You aren't afraid to use that?"

"No." I laughed grimly. After what I'd just seen, I'd have welcomed a chance to hit him between the eyes with the poker.

It was dead silent in the room, except for the ticking of the clock and Monique's breathing.

"Oh no." *Ella.*

"What?" Nicholas glanced at me over his shoulder.

"I have to warn Ella. He could be going after her. He was angry with Monique for helping Sydney."

Monique was watching me with large, frightened eyes. I turned to her. "Did you actually help Sydney?"

She just nodded.

Of all the things I'd expected tonight, this revelation was not one of them.

"Look, you be careful," said Nicholas.

"Of course. May I take the poker?"

"Take it with my blessing. Don't worry, I'll watch over Monique."

"You're a pal." I leaned over and kissed his cheek. "I'll come back if I can."

I dashed out of the doorway before I could think any harder about what I was going to do. The last place I'd seen Ella was a library adjacent to the ballroom.

I pushed my way through the crowd, weaving in and out, no longer observing who I passed, my mind only on Ella and her golden hair and black dress as my eyes passed over the partygoers.

The door to library was closed.

Without hesitation, I seized the handle and shoved it open.

"Ella?" I shouted.

The room was empty.

I nearly turned around in that moment and left, but then I heard my name, called faintly as if from far away.

"Ella!" I called back.

My name came again, from the far end of the room. I tore over to the bookshelves, ripping the books off, throwing them to the floor behind me.

"Ella!"

I gripped the edges of the bookshelves and pulled.

One gave, swinging open.

The room behind was strange. Ivy-covered and strewn with dried, dead flowers. Lanterns hung on the walls, lighting the dark.

And the faerie-beast stood in the middle of the room, one iron arm around Ella, the other pressed over her mouth.

"Don't take another step," he warned. His eyes roamed over my face, as if searching me for emotion. Well, he wasn't going to get any, unless it was pure anger.

Ella's eyes were frightened.

"You have a knack for butting in, Constance Hanover."

"It's Miss Hanover."

"This is my house." He smiled, and there was something wrong between his normal smile and his hungry eyes. "I say what I like."

"It's not your house either!"

"Ella, tell her." He uncovered her mouth with a nasty smile.

She shook her head and her eyes met mine. *Find Leone,* she mouthed.

"I forget sometimes that you really are just a girl." The lawyer shook his head. "It's a pity, really."

"Sydney will save me," Ella spat back.

"Your brother will do nothing of the kind. Haven't you wondered why he didn't come for you all this summer? This house is woven tight with traps and spells. If your brother were to set foot in this house, he would feel as if his hands were aflame and he would collapse in five minutes from weakness. This is my house."

"Sydney knows how to undo such spells."

"Only with months of time," said the lawyer. "And he doesn't have that kind of time."

"He is far cleverer than you."

The lawyer chuckled. "Not this time."

The sound of a door being opened stopped us all.

"Leone!" Ella screamed. "Leone!"

The secret door had been left open. Leone came dashing through, his eyes taking in the scene in a matter of seconds.

"Let her go," he demanded.

"You don't know what's going on here, boy. Take a step back."

"It's me you want, isn't it?" Leone said appeasingly.

"No, it isn't. I want Sydney and Ella Whittingon. I will end them as I ended their parents before them."

Ella blanched.

Leone's eyes flicked to Ella's and a brief look of reassurance crossed his face.

"So you were the one who popped the old man off."

"Leone!" gasped Ella.

"It's not your concern," the lawyer said.

"Oh, I think it is, with the police inspector out there."

"This isn't about the police," snapped the lawyer. "It was personal. I and my kind had the run of this house and its passageways before that man used them for himself and brought back the queen as his wife. She saw to it that we were banished, all but me. For that, I swore I'd end their line forever."

Leone took another step towards the lawyer.

"Stand back! I said I have no quarrel with you, boy."

"Well, you have Ella. Therefore, my quarrel is with you."

"You don't want to do that. I will kill you and take her anyway. Same with you, Constance Hanover, if you continue to get in my way."

Leone reached up and undid his tie, dropping it on the ground.

He smiled, his narrow rogue's grin. "I may as well make you work for it."

He rushed in, right at the lawyer's throat.

Ella screamed and fell as the two crashed to the ground.

"Ella, quick!" I seized her hand and dragged her

towards me as she scrambled up out of reach. The two of them were locked arm to arm, struggling.

The lawyer threw Leone off hard, ten feet away into a wall, and I saw the flash of a knife in his hand.

"Get out of here!" Leone shouted to us.

I did not give Ella a chance to react. I pulled her out of the room and shoved her against a wall, behind me.

"He might kill him," whispered Ella.

"Stay where you are. You can't help him."

"I might." One small fist was knotted.

Horrible sounds of crashing and blows followed. I snatched up a chair and held it in case I needed to use it. It might not do much good against the faerie-beast's strength, but it could buy Ella time to run out the door.

She was gripping my arm like a vice. I knew it was no good convincing her to leave. It was better, anyhow, to keep her with me.

A hard, sudden grunt came from the other room, and Ella gasped, covering her mouth.

I couldn't tell which one had made the sound.

Mentally I retraced the way to the parlor where Nicholas was—no—better, the police inspector. But I didn't know where to find him.

Still, I didn't know if anyone would be able to take the lawyer at his full strength. I had never felt anything quite like that.

A shiver went through my whole body.

Slowly, footsteps came from the other room and Leone, his suit jacket torn and stained, came out.

"He's gone," he said quietly, reaching up and closing the bookcase.

"Gone?"

"He won't come after you ever again." He reached out his hand and took Ella's, drawing her into his arms. "Not ever."

"Are you hurt?" she asked, muffled against him.

"Not in any way that counts. He didn't hurt you?"

"No."

"Miss Hanover?" His glance came to me, and he looked less of a boy and more of a man than I'd ever seen him look before.

"I'm fine."

"Here, you're bleeding." Ella reached up with her handkerchief and wiped a smear of blood from his forehead.

"Is it bad?" He reached up and touched it.

"No. It'll stop. Pull your hair down, just here."

"Now?" He adjusted it blind.

"Perfect."

"Are you ready?" He slipped his suit jacket off his shoulders and cuffed up his white sleeves.

"Ready for what?" Ella glanced from him to me,

confused.

"We're having our last dance."

"Now?"

"That's when we planned it."

"Leone, please, we don't need to."

"I insist. I have been looking forward to it all night."

He took her hand in his and led her to the doorway.

"Miss Hanover?" He turned to look at me, and I swear I saw tears in his eyes. "Thank you."

"Constance." I held out my hand and he clasped it.

As soon as he'd dropped my hand, Ella threw her arms around me and held me in a tight hug. I'd have been shocked if the night had not already been so strange. I'm afraid I just stood there stiffly.

Finally, she let me go.

"After you?" Leone offered.

I stepped through the doorway before them, but I could still catch the edge of their words behind me.

"This is our last time," Leone whispered. "Let's make it one they won't forget."

"I don't care about being remembered," she replied, with a soft laugh. "I'd rather they forgot me and this season altogether."

"Then we'll do it for the fun of the thing."

He led her out into the ballroom, past me as I looked for a place to stand away from the spinning couples.

Inspector Rothschild was standing against the wall; he saw me and moved over a couple feet to give me space. His drink was gone, his arms folded across his chest as his eyes scanned the ballroom.

"Ladies and gentlemen!" Leone stepped out onto the ballroom floor, raising his hand for quiet. "Clear the floor for a moment, please."

The dancers moved slowly towards the walls, leaving Leone standing alone on one end of the floor.

"Thank you all very much for coming tonight. I know, I know—I am not your host, I am not the lovely Ella Whittington. But I wanted us to take a moment and thank her for this beautiful party. I think it may very well be the highlight of the season."

Applause rippled across the room.

"As you all know, this is a going-away party. We are losing our light after this evening, as dear Ella Whittington goes abroad."

A rather sad collective murmur rose in response.

"But—the night is not over yet. I want to ask our dear hostess to join me in one last dance together."

The room broke out in earnest applause.

Leone held out his hand.

"Ella?"

The music began, quick and heart-stirring. Ella and Leone crossed the floor to each other. His hand found her waist, hers his neck, and they turned slowly, their eyes on each other.

I thought I had been mesmerized watching them before. This was different.

He lifted her like she weighed nothing. She moved as smooth and graceful as a river, up into the air, down to the floor, spinning as he whirled her. She was like music in his hands, like starlight under the ballroom lights, laughing.

I'd never seen her face so radiant. And Leone was all show, his white rogue's smile flashing, his crisp, sharp movements as precise as the beat of the music. And the song—it wrapped them up, swept them around, carried them across the floor.

The music swelled and stopped as Leone dropped sharply to one knee, sweeping Ella's head inches from the floor.

Applause rose around me in a muted rush as the ballroom cheered.

Ella looked at me across the floor, a look so direct and strong and beautiful I had no doubt who it was meant for.

"Goodbye," she whispered, through smiling lips.

Inspector Rothschild unfolded his arms and lunged forward.

The room plunged into blackness.

Eighteen

It is said that when the Faerie Queen comes home, the first snow falls in memory of her life among the mortals.

—A History of Faerie and the Folk

THE BALLROOM WAS IN AN UPROAR. Women screaming, men shouting for lights, people pressing and shoving against me, frantic in the dark.

I didn't move. I hardly felt it.

That was goodbye. When the lights came back on, I knew Ella would not be there.

My heart was shocked, hollow.

I am not sure I breathed at all.

"Quiet, quiet now!" shouted a strong, deep voice, breaking through the panic. A tiny light sprang up in the center of the floor, illuminating the face of Inspector Rothschild. He had lit a match and was holding it aloft.

"We must remain calm. The lights will be restored in a moment."

He shook his match out.

There was an uneasy sort of murmur, but the panic of a minute ago had subsided. Candles and lanterns were brought in by staff and the room returned to the dim lighting it had before.

"Now listen closely, I need everyone's cooperation and patience." The Inspector was still in the middle of the room, his hands held up placatingly. "This disturbance may have some relevance to police business. I would like to request that each one of you stays where you are and does not leave or roam about the house. Is that understood? Make yourselves comfortable and I will get you home as soon as I reasonably can."

He motioned to a member of the staff and whispered something to him. The man nodded, gesturing out into the hall, and they left together.

We waited, I the most patient of a disturbed, milling crowd. Surely there were others who were now trapped in other rooms, but the ballroom seemed to contain most of the crowd.

I didn't see Colonel Streatfield anywhere.

Even though I knew it was useless, my eyes searched the crowd for Ella or even Leone. Every black dress, every golden head with hair piled high raised my hopes for a split second.

But I knew, deep down, when she'd said goodbye that I wasn't going to be seeing her again.

After a while, Albert Rothschild returned, a half dozen colleagues in tow, and they began to go systematically through all of us, identifying each person and letting them out one by one.

I passed Rothschild himself, and he gave me a nod and jerked his head for me to pass. It paid, I guess, to be friendly to the man with no friends.

I went straight to the room out front where I'd left Nicholas and Monique.

Nicholas was sitting on a chair in the middle of the room, his cane across his lap, his eyes on the doorway.

"Nicholas?"

"Constance!" He stood up to greet me. "Something must have happened. The lights went completely out and we never saw the faerie-beast."

"Yes. I am sorry I couldn't have come sooner."

"That's all right, though I was starting to wonder if I'd be seeing you again."

"I'm sorry. There was—" My mind just stopped

short rather than try to recall everything that had just happened.

"Is Ella all right?"

"I—I think so." I didn't know what to think. "The faerie-beast is gone."

"Ah."

"Where is Moniuqe?"

"In the corner."

Monique was asleep on the couch under the window, Nicholas's jacket draped over her bare shoulders.

"Is she all right?"

"Yes. Just exhausted."

"Poor darling. I wanted to tell her that everything was all right. I'd never seen her so frightened."

"Do you want me to wake her?"

"No. Just tell her there is no longer anything to worry about."

"I will. And don't worry about her. I'll make sure she gets home."

"Thank you." I threw my arms around him and hugged him tightly. "I can't tell you what an absolute dear you are."

He laughed, deep in his throat.

"Constance, you're a finer girl than you give yourself credit for."

· · ·

I stepped out into the hallway, leaving them to the quiet of the room. If I was Monique, I'd probably sleep for two days after that fright. The hallway itself was not too full; a steady but small stream of people passed me, headed from the ballroom and the smoking parlors out the front doors, and every time the door opened there was a gust of cold wind and the sound of automobiles pulling away.

I did not want to be in the middle of the rush, and there was, of course, the matter of the lawyer. I should probably say something to Inspector Rothschild about him.

"Miss?" A young, clean-shaven policeman came up to me, all polite efficiency.

"What is it?"

"I believe this is yours? The Inspector said to look for a tall woman with short dark hair and a long string of pearls."

He held out my clutch.

"Oh, yes." I took it from his gloved hand. "Thank you."

"It was in one of the parlors at the end of the hall."

I must have set it down there when Monique wasn't feeling well, and of course I hadn't given it a second's thought after I'd defied the lawyer to his face.

I opened it up to see if the contents were still inside, and there was the letter Ella had given me at the door. I had forgotten.

The letter was sealed, with "Constance" written in bold ink on the front. I tore it open hastily and unfolded it.

Dearest Constance,

I wish I had been at liberty to say goodbye properly. But you must take this note from me instead and know that with it comes all my love and best wishes. I am sorry I could not tell you that Leone was my brother, Sydney. I did not like, as our friendship grew, to keep that secret from you. But it had to be kept from all. I imagine you can guess where we are going. I do not expect I will ever see you again, and for that I am sorry.

Know that during this season, you gave me, for a short while, the pleasure of knowing what a sister must be like, and that I will always remember you that way.

Though now the paths of our lives must diverge, know that I will think of you often. And if you ever see a burst of daisies where they do not belong, perhaps that will have been me.

Yours ever,

Ella Whittington

I read the letter through thrice. The words would not seem to sink in. Leone—Sydney?

I wandered over to the staircase and sat down, the letter still gripped in my cold fingers.

How was that possible? I'd seen Sydney on stage with his dark hair, his strong jaw, his mature, serious face. And Leone—I knew him so well. Laughing, fair, charming, with green eyes like trouble.

And then I remembered something Ella had said as she had picked the last of the daisies—that the Prince of the faeries, with great effort, could cast a glamor over himself so as to walk among the mortals unrecognized.

But that—I still wasn't sure about that.

The tears in his eyes tonight, the way he took on the faerie-beast, the way he had let Ella hold his hand that night after dinner.

That I could be sure about.

I folded up the letter and tucked it back in its envelope. This was going to take quite some time to think through.

"Are you all right?" Inspector Rothschild came around the side of the staircase and leaned his arms on the rail.

I nodded, slowly.

"Anything the matter? You haven't gone home."

"I suppose I need to get up the strength," I replied languidly.

"You have your automobile?"

"Yes."

"Drive yourself?"

I nodded.

"Tell one of my officers if you need an escort. I don't want you getting in an accident on the way home."

"Thank you."

He nodded brusquely and started to walk away.

"Oh, Inspector?" I called after him.

I had something to show him.

We stood in the small library adjacent to the ballroom and I showed him how the secret door worked while he and three of his men watched.

It gave and began to swing open. I shut it again.

"Are you going in?" The Inspector looked confused.

"No." My voice failed me. Even thinking about what had happened made me feel suddenly weak in my knees. "I can't."

"No?" demanded one of the younger officer.

"Quiet." Rothschild snapped. "Constance, is there a reason?"

I nodded. Like I said, my voice had failed me.

"Clear off, lads." Rothschild waved them off to the far end of the room.

"Do you know what I am going to find in there?" he asked me seriously.

"Only in the vague sense."

"You don't know for sure?"

"I know you'll find someone, and he will be your culprit."

"Is he—"

"Yes," I whispered. "But he confessed in front of me to the killing of Mr. Whittington."

His eyebrows shot up. "Any other witnesses?"

"Ella. And—and Leone." I drew my hand across my forehead. All the nerves and courage that had pounded through my veins for the last few hours were wearing away, and I was so very tired.

"Sydney," he corrected quietly.

I turned to look at him as if seeing him for the first time. "How did you guess?"

He rubbed his nose wearily. "I have my ways, and I have been trying to find him all summer and fall." He smiled wryly. "There were a lot of rumors around that family."

"Mr. Simmonds did say some rather strange things about Ella's father."

"What, that he married a faerie queen?"

"What?"

Rothschild laughed, the kind of laugh that comes

out when you are so tired you simply cannot help your-self anymore. "I have been in the force a very long time, and sometimes gossip must be my business."

"Was she?"

"How am I to know? But if Mr. Simmonds—" He nodded towards the room. "Anyway. Please stay here for a little while longer, just in case a question comes up. I won't need a statement tonight."

He took a deep breath as if pulling together his courage again, and he went through the bookshelves to the secret room.

I dragged the chair I'd picked up for my defense just hours ago into one corner of the room and made myself as comfortable as I could. My hands were beginning to shake.

The low murmur of voices reached me through the open door, but I could only hear their tones and not the words.

One of the younger officers came out in a hurry and passed through into the ballroom. The hum of voices continued, and a couple minutes later, the officer who'd left returned with three more men.

I waited for what seemed like an hour, and then a body, completely covered, was carried out on a stretcher. There was blood on the sheet covering him.

At last, Inspector Rothschild came out.

"Pardon me one moment," he said, and left the room.

When he returned, he was unchanged save that his hands were wet and his tie had been straightened.

"Miss Hanover, you are free to go. Thank you for your assistance."

I nodded, in a daze. "Is—is everything all right?"

"I imagine so. That man in there was...not quite human. It agrees with the evidence I have so far, and I will need to do some more digging before the verdict is final, but I think he told you the truth."

"And Ella and—Sydney?"

"They're gone, I think. No sign of them."

"Do you believe it? What happened?"

"Miss Hanover, I am a man of facts. You would be surprised with how often the facts support the unimaginable."

I just nodded, vaguely, trying to turn that sentence in my head, sort out its truth for myself.

"I will call at your house in a few days, if that is acceptable, and get your statement. No need to come down to the station."

"Thank you."

"Goodnight." He gave me a smile, a real one meant for me this time, not just a polite formality.

· · ·

I asked the first of the staff I ran across to get my coat and things and to have my automobile brought to the door. And I waited in the front hall where Ella had greeted me just hours ago. Those things, so true and real, were now just ghosts of memories.

Most of the guests had gone already, but the rooms in the house were still lit. It had taken hours for them to get the electric lights back on, and now it was going to take nearly as much work to turn them all off again.

"Here you are." A girl handed me my coat and fur ruff. "Sorry for the wait, ma'am."

I just gave her a nod and put them on.

My automobile was idling out front, puffing in the cold air, in the world of white.

But it wasn't until I stepped out onto the front steps that I realized—it was snowing. Snowing beautiful, white flakes over the trees and the paving stones, filling the velvet blue of the night.

It was the first snow. The snow that falls when the Faerie Queen comes home.

Nineteen

Remember, though Faerie takes pains to remain hidden, it shows itself in many beautiful, ordinary ways: the bubbling of a brook, the scattering of wildflowers, the dancing of fireflies. The greatest power of the folk of Faerie is to spread beauty and goodness wherever they go.

—A History of Faerie and the Folk

I SLEPT until one o'clock the next afternoon. Mother said she had never seen me so tired. I'd come home just after three, left the automobile right in front of the house, and stumbled upstairs with some strange smile on my face.

And then slept until the sun had melted away every evidence of the snow from the night before, except for little patches caught under the shade of the ornamental trees and bushes.

"I am hearing all sorts of talk and scandal from last night," my mother informed me as I ate my breakfast and she observed me with a cup of tea.

"Last night there was all manner of scandal," I agreed. "But parties are often that way."

"It's not every time the police are called."

I wiped the corner of my mouth with my napkin and folded it. "Thankfully, the police did their job."

"Was anyone arrested? There is talk that Sydney Whittington may have been there."

"No one was arrested." I got up from the table and collected my plates.

"Leave those for the servants, Constance, it's all right. No one was hurt, that you saw?"

My mind went immediately to the lawyer. To the shrouded stretcher. I shuddered, setting the dishes back down on the table with a soft clink.

For some reason the clink and the soft sunshine filtered through the dining room curtains were the most real thing to me in that moment.

"One or two, but nothing that wasn't handled."

"And you were not hurt? You seem unlike yourself."

Gentler, perhaps? Certainly I was not in the usual mood I displayed to Mother, ill-tempered and resistant.

"No, I don't think so."

I wandered out of the dining room and across the hall to the library, looking for that blue-and-white bound volume.

A History of Faerie and the Folk.

I pulled it off the shelves and started up the stairs.

"Are you sure you are all right, Constance?" Her face was worried.

I tucked the volume under my arm and turned to face her. There were more lines in her face, more gray strands in the stern black of her tight bob. A change in her demeanor that you wouldn't notice except here, a mere two feet away, looking her in the eyes.

Losing Marge took something from her.

"Yes." I gave her a little smile. Not much, but genuine. "I will be upstairs reading. It was a trying night, if nothing else."

"Good. Rest is—good." She was confused, I think. "Dinner will be at seven tonight. Your father will be home. We can eat together?"

"I'll be there."

. . .

The next morning, just after sunrise, my mother called up the stairs.

I was still half asleep, the book I'd been up reading most of the night left open on my bedstand like a promise of a better future.

"Constance, you have a delivery in the hall!"

I went to my door, pulling my dressing gown over my arms. "What is it?"

"Flowers. Is there an admirer you haven't told me about?"

"No." I tied it solidly and headed downstairs.

On the front hall table was a small glass vase filled with snowdrops, and propped up against it, a letter with my name on it.

I tore open the envelope and scanned down the words for a name. When I found it, I stopped short.

"Is it an admirer?" my mother called from the other room.

"No. Just—a friend, I think."

I started the letter from the beginning.

Constance,

I hope that you do not think me forward, writing you this way after acting like a rake all summer long. It was an unwilling role, but a necessary one, and I hope, in the end, one you will forgive me for.

I must thank you for looking out for my sister. My

hope of taking Ella home to our mother's world was a long-standing point of contention between my father and I, and sadly, the subject of our quarrel the night he died. But her well-being was a goal we had in common, and I know he would have wanted to thank you too. You may never know the things your presence shielded her from. For my sister to have one person in the world from whom she did not have to protect herself, or whose presence would not draw the attention of those who wanted her harm, meant more to me than anything.

When I first met you this summer, I could see that you were different. Not simply that you were tired of the shallow pleasures society extends, but that something true had torn a hole in the illusion of this life, and you could no longer reconcile everything you saw or thought to be true. I am sorry that it had to be the loss of your sister.

Snowdrops are considered among my people to be a symbol of hope after loss. It could be of a person, or a dream, or simply a regret one feels over something that cannot be gotten back. They are also a symbol of new beginnings. I hope that you will take them as a sign of my gratitude and consider both meanings to come straight from my heart.

I hope that at last you will find the peace and solace

you seek. Not all things that are lost are lost forever, and not all goodbyes remain bitter.

—Sydney

The talk of the disappearance was everywhere for the next couple weeks, and the gossip was atrocious. No one knew truly what had happened, except for the few of us. Of those few, fewer knew that Sydney was expected that night, and fewer still knew the lawyer's fate. After giving my statement, I never heard another thing, not from the police or in the papers.

For all the public knew, Leone and Ella had eloped with the money and would never return.

As for Monique, she came over to my house for tea the week after the incident. She'd hugged me as if I was an old friend.

"Constance, darling, you will never guess." Her face was aglow—I could guess. I had only ever known one thing to make her glow like that.

But as we sat down together, I told her I could not.

"Nicholas drove me home the other night in his car. It was so late and I knew that my aunt was going to be worried to death, and he talked with me the whole way home and let me tell him all about everything that had happened, and by the time I got home, I wasn't nearly so frightened anymore."

"I am glad to hear it."

I picked up a strawberry ice and began to eat it, motioning for her to proceed.

"And when he left, he asked if he might take me to the city for dinner some night."

"Did you tell him yes?"

Her voice went soft. "I did. And he took me. Oh, Constance, I already know that I love him."

"Does he want to see you again?"

She nodded. "We talked for hours. He likes to talk about real things, about life and hope and what the names of the stars are."

Monique took a sip of her tea. "Did you know, Constance, I thought all men needed me to be pretty and shallow and talk about fashion and shopping and gossip? Except for Sydney, of course, and we had to pretend." She sighed.

"So the jilting was planned?"

She nodded, a little sadly.

"Besides Nicholas, he was the greatest gentleman I'd ever met. It was worth pretending and losing him. And spying for him. He was so respectful when we were in private."

"When do you see Nicholas again?"

Her face lit again, thoughts of Sydney left behind. "Tomorrow."

As we said goodbye that afternoon, I clasped her hands and wished her all the best, and I truly meant it.

There was one sad casualty in the whole business: Albert Rothschild lost his job. The police department could not present the truth to the community without losing face, and someone had to take the fall for their failure to arrest Sydney Whittington. They forced him to retire and gave him a small pension to soothe their consciences. Word was that he planned to move away from the area, where the scandal wouldn't follow him.

I saw him at a dinner a few weeks later, a small affair hosted by the colonel. He was in one of the side rooms and I'd come in to get a glass of champagne.

He gave me a polite nod as he put a cigarette to his lips and lit a match.

I hadn't known if I should say anything when I first saw him, but we'd become comrades of an unwilling sort, and I didn't want him to leave without knowing my thoughts.

"Inspector Rothschild?"

"Mm?" He looked up, catching the cigarette in his fingers and taking it out of his mouth, the end glowing.

"I am sorry, about that police business."

His face was tired, lined, his eyes a little dead, but my apology brought a small spark into them.

"I am too. For the way it happened. You'd think after thirty years in the force, they'd—" He laughed through his nose and took a pull on his cigarette.

"It was cruel and unfair and entirely inappropriate."

"Well, it's really their loss," he said, staring wearily at the corner of the table. "You can't have everything your way, and at least they're putting me out to pasture, not putting me in front of a firing squad."

I laughed wryly. "And out to pasture cannot all be bad?"

"No." He reached out and crushed the rest of his cigarette in a tray, as if he'd lost his taste for it. "As a man you want to be everything for the ones you love, but—" He gave a little jerk of his head. "The time comes when you realize they're enough."

"I hope your pension covers a cottage?"

"It'll cover that, sure."

"Constance?" It was Monique's voice, calling.

"Good." I picked up my glass. It was strange to think that after the summer we'd had together, my goodbye should just be a little smile. I didn't expect I'd ever see him ever again.

"Miss Hanover," he called after me.

"Yes?" I paused in the doorway and turned back.

"I was there, you know—at your sister's accident."

My fingers stilled upon the door frame.

"She seemed like a girl who was full of life. You must have been fond of each other, and it must have been, must be, hard." His eyes met mine and I was struck with how gentle they were. "I am sorry."

"Thank you." The words fell from my numb lips, and for the first time, I meant them. With all the gratitude in my heart.

We gave each other a nod goodbye, and that was it.

I forgot about Monique calling. My drink was set down somewhere, but I don't remember setting it down at all.

I stepped outside in the cold, still night. My chest was caught in the strangest feeling, straining, as if trying to reach out arms to something even it didn't know.

And then it hit me, like the break of an ocean swell.

It shouldn't have been like this. Marge and I didn't get along, but somewhere deep down, I wished we had and I was so angry that we didn't. Everything she did made me angry. Angry that we didn't love or care for the same things, that she was shallow and foolish, that I wouldn't bend enough to try to meet her until—she wasn't anymore.

And that she never had the chance to change. That even if I changed, she would never see it.

I hated her so much because somewhere deep down I loved her. And all the unfeeling walls I'd built, all the anger I felt, were a vain attempt to keep away the pain I should have felt. The true grief I wished I could feel.

In that moment, I had the clearest thought I'd had in months.

I hope, deep down, you loved me too.

A tear fell down my cheek, hot against the cold, early winter air. The wind whispered through the trees in answer.

Another fell. My eyes filled with tears, overtaking me completely. They streamed down my face as I stumbled towards the garden, its ornamental trees and bushes wrapped in burlap for winter.

I sat down on a cold wooden bench, covered my face, and sobbed my heart out.

Months of grief, of regret, of hate towards Marge, broke apart and fell from my shoulders as I wept and wept and wept.

I had never felt such relief in my life as those tears were to me in that moment. My world, hard and cracked and hopeless, was melting away into a settled sort of peace inside me.

I hadn't known that I wasn't Constance until now.

At last, the tears gave way to a distant calm. I just sat and watched the stars above me, and wondered how many of them had names that only the faeries knew.

"Miss Hanover?" It was the old colonel himself, coming out without a coat, a lantern held aloft that illuminated half of his narrow face. "Are you all right?"

I was frozen.

But I nodded. At long last, I knew I was going to be all right.

Mother made me tea and sent me to soak in a hot bath, like she did when I was little. I didn't mind.

As I sat and let the stinging heat bring life back into my frozen body, I thought of the summer, of the blazing autumn, and of Ella, beautiful Ella with her golden hair.

I will forever remember her laugh in the summer night upon the terrace, the way it lit up the dusk. I will always remember how she treated each person as if they were important, because I think she truly believed they were. And I will remember how everyone believed that wild boy would only bring trouble down on his own head, while all the time he was laying down everything he loved for his queen. And no one would ever know that. They'd believe one version of him to be murderer, the other a liar.

I remembered then something the Shabby Lord had said—about Sydney having the blessings of the faeries in his hands.

I wouldn't be surprised if the colonel had known the secret all along.

They are gone and they will not be back. I even hope—I think—that they will never come back. There's a kind of courage to be found in knowing there is beauty and happiness that this world's cares cannot touch. But I think about them all the time.

Ella didn't want to be remembered, and for all that he was a brilliant showman, I think perhaps Sydney didn't either.

That's just as well, I suppose, because people won't. Time will pass, and they will find a new darling and a new scandal, and they will forget.

I used to think people were callous. Some are. But I think most of them simply don't know. They haven't a clue what's out there. They look at the world the way we look at the sun glittering off the bay and think only of sailboats and swimming costumes and not of wrecks and the countless dead in the deep.

That is how I had been.

Sometimes it takes pain and sorrow to make us see how wonderful the real world is.

But more powerful than pain, I think, is beauty. It

can break our hearts more than sorrow can, because it is more lasting. After pain and sorrow end, there is still beauty.

I wonder, sometimes, if beauty might be a matter of life and death after all.

I had a bouquet of flowers tucked into one arm, my coat and fur ruff wrapped around my neck, my boots on for walking through the snow.

"Where are you going, my dear?"

My mother looked up from her book in the front parlor, where she could read and keep an eye on the household comings and goings.

"To the cemetery. It's time I took a turn."

"Why, Constance, that is very considerate of you."

"Hardly," I replied over my shoulder.

I should have done it long before.

The snow fell gently over the rolling hills of the cemetery, coating the trees and masking new and old graves alike. I knew where it was; I'd been for the funeral. Not since, but I don't easily forget. Mother and Father had put her near but not quite under a fine stand of pine trees.

There was something romantic about it in their minds.

I dusted the snow off the top of the ornate headstone stone, brushed the pine needles off the edges.

Margaret Hanover. Her dates. Beloved daughter and sister.

I'd hated those words when Mother chose them, hated the implication that I had to be sorry, that she been something beloved to me.

I pulled the letter out of my pocket and unfolded it.

Marge,

These words are long in coming. Forgive me for the time it took to find them. You know well that we did not get along for most of our lives, and we ended our time together in angry words.

I believe with all my heart that if we'd known the future, we would have made different choices. And I would have told you that afternoon that I loved you.

Though it is too late to say it now, I hope that somehow you knew.

Yours,

Constance

I lit a match and let the letter burn, the ashes flying away on the wind.

The only answer was the wind in the pines,

sweeping the snow off the heavy boughs and scattering it over us both like a fresh snowfall.

I laid the bouquet down over her grave, a small piece of life persisting in the middle of gray desolation.

"I hope you like them," I whispered.

They were snowdrops. They suited her.

Acknowledgments

To Elisabeth, for her untiring work and ability to see the shine in the unpolished diamond. Thanks for being there.

To James Egan, for the stunner of a cover. I am often rendered speechless when I get your mockups and this was no exception. Thanks for making me look so good.

To the Inkwell, for their many encouragements, prayers, gifts, and sweet words. I couldn't pick a better crew to navigate the author life with.

To Lydia, for loving this book from the very start. Thanks for keeping the fire lit.

To my fellow Inklings, Victoria Yu, Christopher Hammond, and Chris Wach, for your help, encouragement, and time spent sharing life at an instrumental point in this book's creation. Without you, this story would not have had the same meaning.

To Liz Koetsier, Cindy Worrell, Taylor Halstead, Hannah Bryson, and many others who at various times offered their prayers and encouragement. You guys are the best.

To my street team, always ready to be there and share, thank you for all the help and enthusiasm.

To my proofreaders, Anna and Lucy, whose zeal and skill were definitely a blessing to this author. Much thanks.

To my kind and loving Heavenly Father, who delights to call me his. It is surprising how often facts support the unimaginable. Thank you for making me a storyteller.

EMILY HAYSE is a lover of log cabins, strong coffee, NASCAR, and the smell of old books. Her writing is fueled by good characters and a lifelong passion for storytelling. When she is not busy turning words into worlds, she can often be found baking, singing, or caring for one of the many dogs and horses in her life. She lives with her family in Michigan.